THE MASKED SAINT

"As a kid growing up, my heroes in life were Tonto and the Lone Ranger, the masked rider of the plains! I just discovered another lone ranger: Chris Whaley. If you're in need of encouragement and you love it when truth overcomes evil and when the underdog rallies to pull out a win, you're going to love *The Masked Saint*. It's a good one."

—**Dr. Kevin Leman**, *New York Times* best-selling author.

"Having read *The Masked Saint* by Chris Whaley, I can commend this book to you as an enjoyable and sometimes humorous recounting of a young pastor's life and ministry—even though his life and ministry follow a different path than most. His style and presentation encourage believers to put away prejudices and to accept the life-transforming power of our Lord, Jesus Christ. I commend this book to you and pray you will enjoy it as I did."

—**Dr. Frank Page**, President, Southern Baptist Convention, 2006–2008, President and CEO – Southern Baptist Convention Executive Committee

"Body-slamming a deserving criminal? Now that is a fleeting image to which almost every pastor can confess. Whaley, a former professional wrestler turned Baptist pastor, gives us an entertaining and fictional peek at what might happen if pastors actually did some of the things they wished they could do. Many a pastor will sympathize readily with this shrouded champion who rights wrongs and defends the defenseless— though the Scriptures prevent us all from imitating his costumed combat in real life."

—**Dr. Paige Patterson**, President, Southwestern Baptist Theological Seminary, Fort Worth, Texas

"For his maiden voyage as an author, Chris Whaley has produced a superb piece of work. He has a vocabulary that is readable and a style that uses review and preview to perfection. Writing as a minister, he captures great truth in a pragmatic way. This is an excellent read for parents and young people. He brings tributaries of ethics and experience together and forms a river of moral truth. I like it!"

—**Dr. John Sullivan**, Executive Director/Treasurer,
Florida Baptist Convention

"Growing up watching professional wrestling and fulfilling my own dream of wrestling for WCW and the WWF, I always somehow knew the good guy wins in the end! Everyone has a little Chris Whaley in them. Who would have ever thought combining a wrestler with a superhero could be so entertaining? I thoroughly enjoyed this book; he says and does what many of us wish we could do. His honest look at himself and his life is testament to a stand-up guy who loves God and his family. You inspire me, Chris!"

—**Marc Mero**, WWF Intercontinental Champion/Johnny B. Badd/
WCW World Television Champion, Founder, Champion of Choices

"Everyone has a story. My friend Chris Whaley tells his with humor, transparency, honesty, and insight. His is a unique story of God's grace and faithfulness. He shares both the joys and challenges of serving Christ. I believe spiritual seekers, committed believers, and church leaders will all be encouraged by his story. There are lessons to learn and principles to glean from this journey of faith. Thanks, Chris, for pulling off the mask and letting us inside."

—**Dr. Willie Rice**, President, Florida Baptist Convention,
2007, 2008, 2015 President, Southern Baptist Pastor's Conference

"A novel about a wrestler turned Baptist preacher brought to mind a few real-life church business meetings I've witnessed where the pastor may have wished he could employ the moves of The Masked Saint! Although *The Masked Saint* exposes the sinfulness all too common in churches, Chris Whaley's entertaining novel intersperses those sad episodes with encouraging lessons of God's grace—often from the lips of a common, yet profound, elderly woman. It turns out, the Masked Saint is no superhero; like the rest of us, he is a sinner saved by grace, seeking to share that message of hope with other sinners in need of a Savior. That's what makes *The Masked Saint* a novel all can enjoy."

—**Dr. James A. Smith**, Executive Editor, *Florida Baptist Witness*

"Chris Whaley reminds us that pastors, like many of us, have previous lives of varying backgrounds. His first book, *The Masked Saint*, presents a fictional account of a professional wrestler turned pastor as he confronts right against wrong and good versus evil. When the final bell rings, we find ourselves in his corner."

—**F. Robert Radel II**, JD, Butler Pappas, Tampa, Florida

"Chris Whaley has written a fascinating adventure of a man coming to grips with who he is and who God is. It is challenging, entertaining, and heartwarming. Every pastor and every man should read this book!"

—**Patrick Moody**, former Hollywood actor/director.

"A fascinating story with colorful characters and a story theme that warms the heart."

—**Dr. Paul R. Corts**, President, Council for Christian Colleges and Universities, former Assistant Attorney General

THE MASKED
SAINT

Inspired By True Events
Husband, Pastor, Hero

CHRIS WHALEY

New York

THE MASKED SAINT

Inspired By True Events — Husband, Pastor, Hero

Published in New York, New York, by Morgan James Publishing. Morgan James and The Entrepreneurial Publisher are trademarks of Morgan James, LLC.
www.MorganJamesPublishing.com

The Morgan James Speakers Group can bring authors to your live event. For more information or to book an event visit The Morgan James Speakers Group at
www.TheMorganJamesSpeakersGroup.com.

Scripture comes from the New King James Version®. Copyright © 1982 by Thomas Nelson. Used by permission. All rights reserved.

Shelfie

A **free** eBook edition is available with the purchase of this print book.

CLEARLY PRINT YOUR NAME ABOVE IN UPPER CASE

Instructions to claim your free eBook edition:
1. Download the Shelfie app for Android or iOS
2. Write your name in **UPPER CASE** above
3. Use the Shelfie app to submit a photo
4. Download your eBook to any device

ISBN 978-1-63047-796-7 paperback
ISBN 978-1-63047-797-4 eBook
Library of Congress Control Number:
2015915679

Cover Design by:
Rachel Lopez
www.r2cdesign.com

Interior Design by:
Bonnie Bushman
The Whole Caboodle Graphic Design

In an effort to support local communities and raise awareness and funds, Morgan James Publishing donates a percentage of all book sales for the life of each book to Habitat for Humanity Peninsula and Greater Williamsburg.

Get involved today, visit
www.MorganJamesBuilds.com

Habitat
for Humanity®
Peninsula and
Greater Williamsburg
Building Partner

This book is dedicated, with love and affection, to my wife, Verna, for her love and support throughout our lives together. You have been my best friend for forty years.

To our two daughters, Alyson and Kacie, who are sunshine to any dark day I have ever had. I wish every parent could have the opportunity to have two children as wonderful as you.

To my sons-in-law, Rob and Bret, who are like a sons to me. You are the answer to a mom and dad's prayer for godly young men to marry their daughters.

To my mom and dad: great parents, wonderful grandparents.

To the late, Great Malenko, who taught me to wrestle. I feared you as a kid and loved you as an adult.

—Chris Whaley

TABLE OF CONTENTS

PREFACE

For years, I dreamed of this book. The idea began in the early 1980s. I never thought I would be the one to write it.

I was inspired by Michael Landon, who gave us the series *The Little House on the Prairie* and *Highway to Heaven*. I have always loved stories of good versus evil (with good coming out on top).

I tried and tried to provide the information to several writers over the years so they might write the book. It never worked. I was destined to write it.

I was a sickly child. I had pneumonia several times, polio, viral encephalitis, and over 192 different allergies.

When I was a kid, there just wasn't much on TV late at night. Because of my many sicknesses, it was not unusual for me to be awake late in the evening. Professional wrestling was one of the few things playing at that hour of the night. I got hooked on wrestling.

I answered an ad in the paper in 1978: Wanted: Professional Wrestlers. I was hooked the moment I walked into the gym. Wrestling is very different today than it was then; I prefer then.

Wrestling gave me opportunities I normally would never have had. As an oddity (a seminary student who was also a professional wrestler), I was given many opportunities to speak all across the southeastern United States. Even though I got out of wrestling in 1988, it never got out of my system.

It is a miracle and testimony to what God can do that I even got the chance to enter the squared circle. It is an even greater miracle that God called me into the ministry.

The Masked Saint is also a feature film based on this incredible story. Full of suspense and drama, the film shows the power of God to fight our battles for us.

Visit www.TheMaskedSaint.com to watch the trailer, download a Bible study, and learn more about the film. You can also use your smart phone and scan this QR code to get there faster:

FOREWORD

Chris Whaley is the very person to write *The Masked Saint* because much of the book reflects his own experiences. Whaley, whom I have known for thirty-five years, has always seethed when the poor, needy, misrepresented, or unrepresented have been mistreated, used, or abused.

He loves the underdog and writes his own psychodrama through the characters who parade through these pages.

It's a great read for young people, as well as those of all ages.

The Masked Saint is very much like the Saturday afternoon movie serials I watched at the old Palace Theater every Saturday afternoon back in the late thirties. My young eyes danced in excitement as the hero was put in a hopeless situation—only to be extricated through his own cunning.

Relax, read, and enjoy. You will find quiet release through the moves of Chris Whaley's Masked Saint!

—**Dr. Jess C. Moody**, former pastor of The Shepherd of the Hills Church, Porter Ranch, California, Founder and first President, Palm Beach Atlantic University

CHAPTER ONE
STARTING OVER

I t was difficult to think that at thirty years of age, I was about to start all over again. Most people in Florida would have given their left arm for all I had. I left a new home on the lake. My wife left her job teaching at her alma mater to allow me to pursue the calling of God on my life. We left all we knew, and with our two little girls, we moved fifteen hundred miles away to Southwestern Baptist Theological Seminary in Fort Worth, Texas.

We lived in what we called "The Gospel Ghetto," which was located on the campus of the seminary. The home was so small, I could stretch out in the living room and my feet would be in the bathroom. Even though it had a musty smell and you could feel the cold air blowing through the wall on a winter night, it was home.

I entered seminary at the age of thirty. Most of the students were in their early twenties. Not only did I feel the difference because I was older than most of the students, but my size was also noticeable. Guys who look like bodybuilders look different from the average seminary student. I was not the average seminary student. I was a seminary student who was also a professional wrestler.

During orientation in my first week of seminary life, I heard the vice president say, "Don't ever embarrass the seminary."

When I had an opportunity to talk with him, I said, "Sir, you said we were never to embarrass the seminary. I have to work to provide for my family, and you might consider what I do for a living to be an embarrassment to the school."

"Oh," he said, "just exactly what is it that might be an embarrassment to our school?"

"Well, sir, I am a professional wrestler."

He laughed and said, "No, seriously, what is it you do?"

"I'm a professional wrestler, sir."

My outlook on my future at seminary was greatly encouraged on that day. I'll never forget his words. That learned man, who was respected as a theological academician, said, "Son, if you do it the best you can, hopefully you will not embarrass yourself or our great school."

Standing in the dressing room at my locker, memories poured through my mind. I was about to wrestle in my last match before I turned in the tights and mask. I would leave the smell of the arenas and the screaming, passionate fans and enter the opposite end of the spectrum in life. Soon, we would be moving back to Florida, and I would no longer be The Gladiator. I would be Reverend Chris Samuels.

"Hey, Sam, you ain't still going to quit rasslin, are you?" His name was Ed, but his ring name was The Terminator. He was a former college football player at the University of Alabama. Today was Saturday, and it was college football season. And much to everyone in the locker room's dismay, Alabama was playing against Tennessee on the television in the locker room. The crowd on TV roared, and Ed quickly turned around to hoop and holler over the Tide getting a first down.

"I don't know if you guys remember; I played at Alabama!"

I couldn't resist the moment, so I said, "I knew you were an Alabama grad."

"How did you know that?" he responded, surprised.

"I saw your class ring while you were picking your nose."

Everyone else in the locker room loved it, but Ed just continued to watch the game, oblivious to my comment.

I quickly laced up my boots and loosened up my muscles. I would be working against the Grim Reaper, a kid who was quickly moving up the ladder of professional wrestling. He was moving up, not because he was good or a crowd pleaser, but because he was built like a Greek god and had the looks to go with it. Even though he was a "bad guy" in wrestling, the promoter would soon be changing his image and turn him into a "good guy."

The only problem working with someone who was "green" (someone who was new to the wrestling profession) was he tended to stiffen up when he got in front of the crowd. It was easy to get hurt working with someone who was new to the business. I had been wrestling for ten years and had learned several years ago how to protect myself.

Soon the promoter would come in and tell both of us how long the match would last and who was going to win. I always wanted to win, but when I was told to put someone else over and let him win, I always did my best. On this night, I was sure hoping to go out a winner.

Everyone in wrestling has a gimmick. The good guys were called "baby faces," and the bad guys were called "heels." Each had a gimmick to match his ring name. I wrestled as The Gladiator. I was the perennial good guy.

Things had changed in the wrestling world from the time I entered the business in 1978. Guys were getting bigger and bigger, and it wasn't because of weight training.

Steroids were becoming a pretty common thing. I was even told one time by a promoter, "Blow your body up, and I'll make a star out of you."

I knew it wasn't for me. Little did I know how big doping would become in the business of professional wrestling. I wasn't the sharpest knife in the drawer, but I always figured the heart was a muscle too. If steroids would make your muscles bigger, I could only imagine what it would do to the heart. Again, it wasn't for me.

The promoter came in and called our names. "Gladiator, I'm getting ready to turn the Reaper into a baby face. I want you guys to go for about twenty minutes. The Terminator is going to interfere in the match."

"Reaper, I want you to grab The Gladiator's arms and walk him over to the ropes. When The Terminator starts to hit The Gladiator, drop down, and he's going to hit you (pointing to the Terminator). Gladiator, after that, get out of the ring, and let them work the crowd."

At least I wasn't going out on the losing end. It was okay with me.

CHAPTER TWO
THE TRIP BACK TO FLORIDA

ifferent denominations call pastors through different methods. Some denominations have hierarchies. The hierarchies usually place pastors in churches. Southern Baptist churches are what we call autonomous (self-governing). Southern Baptists usually have a search committee that finds a pastor for their church.

When I was in my last semester of seminary, I put out my resume. I would go anywhere God called me to go, but I was really hoping I would be able to go back to Florida. Florida was home to me and my wife. I also felt my wife was hoping Florida would be where we would end up. I often joked that my wife said, "I'll go anywhere the Lord calls you—in Florida." But I knew she would go wherever the Lord called.

I received several letters from search committees, telling me they had received my resume, but none of them had contacted me personally to talk with me. Then, it happened. One night while I was studying, the phone rang.

"Reverend Samuels, this is Joe Becton from Auburndale, Florida." My heart sped up a little as I heard the word *Florida*.

"Hello, Mr. Becton, it sure is good to talk with someone from my home state. How are things in the Sunshine State?"

"Things are pretty good here. I hope things are going well for you."

After some other pleasantries, he continued, "I am the chairman of the search committee for the Westside Baptist Church. We got your resume from the seminary and would like to talk with you about coming to be our pastor."

I was so excited; finally, someone was interested in me. We talked for about thirty minutes. I answered his questions and told him I would be graduating very soon. The church wanted us to fly back to Florida as soon as we were able to make the trip. I looked at my calendar, and we settled on a date. My wife and girls were ecstatic when I hung up the phone and shared we would be flying to Florida in two weeks to meet with the committee and talk to the people at the church.

I still had several commitments right up until graduation, but my schedule was open during the time the church wanted me to come to Florida.

My wife had that look on her face that told me something was up. "What's on your mind, babe? You don't look as happy as I thought you would be." I thought I knew what was on her mind, but I would let her tell me.

"Did you tell him what it is you do for a living?"

"No. I'm not planning to tell them. Why do they need to know? I will not be doing it anymore when I graduate and go to a church." *Besides*, I thought to myself, *I wrestle under a mask. No one knows who I am.*

My wife and I have a great relationship. She has been one of God's greatest gifts to me. She has always been supportive of me in everything I have done. I didn't think there was a need to share with the church what I did for a living for ten years of my life. That life was over. Now I would be embarking on what God had called me to do.

The time passed quickly as we anticipated the trip to Florida. My folks lived in the area, and they were excited about us coming home. They would be able to pick us up at the airport. My girls had never flown on a plane and were very excited about their first plane trip.

As I sat at my desk, I thought about Miss Edna, a special lady from my childhood. She would be excited for me too. She was influential in my life when I was trying to figure out if God was calling me into the ministry.

When I was a little boy, sitting in her living room one day, I heard her say something that has stayed with me since that time.

"Child, someone once said, 'The only thing necessary for the triumph of evil is for good men to do nothing.' I've always tried to remember that, child. I don't want to be one of them people that does nothing. I believe God wants all of us to do everything we can to do the right thing. That's what you need to do, child. Always do the right thing."

Even as a little boy, I made the commitment: I would always, to the best of my ability, try to do the right thing.

The day finally arrived for us to leave for Florida. My little girls were so excited. Their grandparents were also very excited as they talked with them the night before we left.

We made our way to the Dallas/Fort Worth International Airport and checked our bags. We walked to our gate to wait for the flight, only to find our flight had been delayed an hour due to bad weather.

Waiting an extra hour didn't bother our girls. Their noses were flush against the window as they watched the planes land and take off. My wife pulled out her book and read to occupy her time. I was too anxious to read, so I decided to walk around and maybe stop in at one of the many stores in our terminal.

As I headed toward a store, there was an elderly man looking at his ticket as he walked. Even though he didn't mean to do it, he bumped right into a couple of men who were on their way out of the terminal. I couldn't believe it as I watched one of the men shove the elderly man and tell him to watch where he was going. My blood always boiled when I saw someone mistreat the elderly.

Even though the elderly man apologized for his blunder, one of the men continued to say unkind things to the poor man. Now my blood was really boiling.

I followed the men as they walked into the restroom. I could hear the men hooting and hollering over the fact they had (in their words), "Set that guy straight."

As I walked into the restroom, I couldn't help but share my views on the matter. "You know, guys, I saw the whole thing happen. That old guy was looking at his ticket. He didn't mean to walk into either of you."

"Who are you? Mr. Goodbody? Why don't you mind your own business?"

Miss Edna came to my mind: "The only thing necessary for the triumph of evil is for good men to do nothing." I don't know if this would rank up there with what she had in mind, but I felt it was.

"Well, guys, I'm here—and there are two of you. Why don't you shove me like you did that old man? But remember, I might not react the same way he did."

I watched the men as they eyed one another. They obviously thought they had the advantage since there were two of them and only one of me. And they obviously were feeling a little cocky after intimidating an old man.

The one who had shoved the old man took a swing at me. I ducked very quickly and saw his fist hit his buddy right square in the jaw, knocking him to the ground. I grabbed him with both hands, picked him up, and pressed him up against the wall.

"Listen, buddy, you can thank a little lady you don't even know that I don't wipe this bathroom floor with you. I suggest you get your friend and get out of my sight as quickly as you can."

He didn't need any more encouragement to leave. He picked his buddy up and proceeded to leave very quickly. It felt good to set things right for the elderly gentleman, even though he didn't know anything about it.

I made my way back to the gate and waited with my girls for our plane to arrive. My wife put her book down and said, "What have you been up to?"

"Oh, just walking around and looking."

We boarded soon afterward and were on our way to F-L-A.

CHAPTER THREE
THE INTERVIEW

My folks were the first faces we saw as we exited the plane. The girls ran to their nanny and papa and jumped in their arms. We exchanged hugs, got our bags, and were on our way to my folks' house. They were excited to hear all about finishing seminary and listening to the girls talk about their school and friends. I hadn't realized how much I missed them and missed home. We had a great evening, talking and catching up with all the news.

My relationship with my mom had always been good. Mom was the one who started our spiritual heritage. She had grown up in a cult. Her dad was very involved in the cult and made the family participate, but my mom always knew things didn't add up. She had longed and prayed for someone to talk with who might help her settle some things in her mind and heart.

After my mom and dad moved to Florida, a local pastor was knocking on doors in the neighborhood one afternoon. He was trying to get to know the people and also invite them to church. When he knocked on our door, my mom told him she had been praying for someone like him to talk with.

My mom was able to ask questions about what she had been taught while she was growing up. The pastor was able to answer all of her questions and at the same time tell her about Jesus. He told her Jesus had died on a cross for her sins and that she could accept him by faith and know the assurance of heaven.

Mom became a Christian that day and became a part of the local church. It was miraculous. Winning someone to Christ who has been raised in a cult is very rare.

My dad was not only a long-distance truck driver, but he was also a "fifth degree redneck." He was quite a barroom brawler. He had very little education, though he was a hard-working man who always tried to do a good job.

He never had a dad at home to teach him how to be a dad or a good husband. He had never been to church very much while growing up. Naturally, he wasn't too thrilled when my mom first started attending the local church.

My dad became a Christian when I was a teenager. His conversion was one of the things that convinced me of the reality of God. I always said, "If God can change my dad, He can change anyone."

He wasn't the greatest father, but he became a wonderful grandfather. He and Mom were both wonderful grandparents.

The next day after we arrived, my wife and I drove to the church for my interview with the search committee. I must admit, my stomach was in knots as we pulled into the parking lot.

I had wrestled some of the biggest and meanest men in the world, but I had never been put in this kind of situation. I took a deep breath as we opened the office door to walk in.

The committee was waiting with coffee and donuts. They all seemed very friendly—just simple, good, country folks. I saw a couple of the men whisper to each other as they sized me up. One of them even said, "You're a little bigger than you look in your resume photo."

They asked me a multitude of questions as we sat around the table. They asked me about my leadership style, preaching style, ministering style, and how I planned to help the church grow. Amazingly, I grew more and more at ease as we continued to talk. They seemed to like me and my answers, but they *loved* my wife.

Many times, when a church calls a pastor, they expect his wife to be as involved in the ministry as the pastor. I assured them my wife would be as involved as the average member of the church, but I also reminded them they were calling *me* as pastor, not my wife. I shared that I was very protective of my family. They seemed to be encouraged by my statement, rather than turned off.

After the meeting, a couple of the committee members showed us around the church grounds. It was a small church, but the facilities were in good shape. I was at ease as we looked around; I felt a great peace that this was where God wanted me to be.

The next day I was to preach a sermon and enjoy a potluck lunch with the members so they could also get to know us. The committee would come back together in the evening and vote to see if they would call me as their new pastor.

I preached with strength and conviction in my first message. The people seemed to relate to my style and seemed to accept me. The lunch was absolutely wonderful. It had been a long time since I had enjoyed a meal like that. People in the South know how to cook!

My family and I were anxious as we waited for the call from the chairman of the committee to share the results of the vote. We packed our bags and visited with my folks. After we received the call from the search committee, we would be flying back to Fort Worth to finish up. The only question was, would we be coming back to Florida or would we be waiting for another call from a different church? I jumped when the phone rang. My voice almost trembled as I answered the phone, "Hello, Chris Samuels speaking."

"Reverend Samuels, this is Joe Becton."

"Hello, Mr. Becton, I've been looking forward to your call."

"Well, Reverend Samuels, this was one of the best meetings we have ever had as long as I have been here—and I grew up in this church. The church voted unanimously to ask you to come and be our pastor. So, I'm asking if you would accept our call."

I looked at my family, who were anxiously looking at me. I gave them a thumbs-up, and my girls started screaming and running around the house, yelling at the top of their lungs: "We're moving to Florida! We're moving to Florida!" My folks and my wife had tears in their eyes as I shared with Mr. Becton that I felt this is exactly where God wanted me to be.

After graduating from seminary, I would be coming back to Florida to be the pastor of the Westside Baptist Church.

CHAPTER FOUR
THE BEGINNING

I was born in 1954 in a small town in South Alabama. My dad was a truck driver. His dad had died when he was three years old. He had to quit school when he was in the fourth grade. My mom was eight years younger than my dad. She finished the seventh grade.

Jobs were scarce during that time, which forced my dad to move his family to Central Florida. He found work driving a truck for a large citrus company. Then he found a job driving long distance. The arrangement left my mom and me alone for long periods of time.

When I was six years of age, my folks moved to a different section of town. It was nothing new; we were used to starting over. It seemed every time the rent was due, my folks moved. However, it looked like this would be a place we would finally be able to settle down for a longer period of time.

There weren't many homes in our new neighborhood; we were one of the first families to move there. Of course, I was looking for someone my age to play with. There was a family directly across from us, but they were a young couple and did not have children. An old couple lived at the end of the street, and the old man had already scolded me for walking across his freshly planted grass seeds.

The home near the main street was an older home. I had not seen anyone who lived there, so I decided to check it out. First I walked in front of the house, hoping someone might see me and come outside. That didn't work. So, I decided to walk down the driveway and whistle loudly; after all, I was a kid. I could always say I was sorry if someone came out and wanted me off his property. But nobody came outside.

Just as I was getting ready to turn around, something caught my eye. There was a garden on the other side of the house, and it looked like someone was there. As I walked toward the garden, a frail, little black lady stood up. I had seen a black person one time, but I had never talked to one. I thought I heard my dad talking about blacks once, but he didn't say very many good things about them. I later tried to talk with my dad about what he had said, but he didn't have anything to say to me about the subject.

The little black lady had a big bonnet on her head and a long-sleeved dress. As I walked toward the garden, she smiled at me. "Hello, child, what's your name?" she said as she continued to work.

"My name is Chris, Chris Samuels. I live down the street."

"My name is Edna Williams, and that's my husband Edgar over there watering."

I turned and saw a tall black man, who looked like a giant to me. He never acknowledged my being there; he continued to water the garden.

"I'm just about through with my work, and I was going to get me a drink of cold water. Would you like a drink of cold water, child?" It was awfully hot and humid, and water sure sounded good to me.

We walked to the screened porch, and I stood at the door. "Come on in, child. I ain't going to bite you." I could see my house from her porch, so I figured it would be okay.

She said, "You wait right here, and I'll be right back."

Mr. Williams continued to water the garden and occasionally picked a few weeds.

As she walked back to the porch and opened the door to her house, the most wonderful aroma hit me. I don't know what she was cooking, but it smelled better than anything I had ever smelled. She sat two glasses of water down on a little table and asked me to sit down.

"So, you're the new family that just moved in. You got any brothers or sisters?"

"No, ma'am, I'm the only one."

"Me and Edgar ain't got any young'uns. I always wanted children, but God never seen fit to give me any."

"Thank you for the water; it was real good. I better be getting back home."

"Well, you be sure and come see me again."

"I will; thank you."

As I walked back home, it sure felt good to make a new friend. They didn't seem any different than anyone else I had ever met. I couldn't possibly realize how important that little lady would become in my life. There would be many, many times when I would sit and talk with her. The things I learned, I have carried for a lifetime.

CHAPTER FIVE

THE MASKED SAINT BEGINS

The first church I pastored was a small, Southern church. Like most churches, it was made up of good people. You always have some folks in churches who give everyone else a bad name—those are the ones who make the headlines. You usually don't hear about the good folks in churches. But let me tell you, there are a lot of good folks in church.

I really enjoyed meeting all the new folks in my first church. I warmed up to most of them pretty quickly. However, there are always folks who keep you at an arm's distance.

One particular young lady intrigued me. She was a young mother with three children. She always seemed to come into the service two minutes late and was usually the first one out the door. Since I always went to the front door after the closing prayer, I always tried to say good-bye when she left. That's the way it went for the first few weeks.

I will never forget the Sunday she did not try to be the first one out the door. On that Sunday, she wore long sleeves and actually wore sunglasses during the worship service. She waited until the last person left and gradually made her way to the door. I stuck out my hand to shake hers. She grabbed my hand with both of hers and just stood there.

When I looked into her face, I noticed tears were coming down her cheeks. I gently lifted her glasses and saw two black eyes. I asked her if I could help, but she said, "No, Pastor, please don't do anything, or it will get worse. Just pray for me." I assured her I would do that.

I couldn't eat my lunch that day as I continued to see the young lady's face. I had seen her husband once when he picked her and the children up after church. He looked like a defensive lineman for a pro football team. He was twice her size. I imagined him beating his young wife, and my stomach churned. I don't think much of a man who would hit a woman.

What could I do to help her? I certainly didn't want to cause her any more trouble than she already was dealing with.

I thought back to my childhood and one of my visits with Miss Edna. She always had a way of helping me when I was in trouble.

When I was in elementary school, I was pretty much a "sickly" looking kid. I had many stays in the local hospital because of pneumonia; I was also allergic to just about everything.

It always seems to be the sickly kid or the "runt" of the litter who attracts the bully in the crowd. It didn't take the bully long to find me. He was a big kid who had failed the previous year of school.

My visits with Miss Edna always seemed to bring a peace I didn't have any other time. On this day, while I visited with her, I was sporting a black eye the bully had given me. At first she didn't say anything. But the longer I stayed, the more she stared at my eye.

"What happened to your eye, child?" I had told my mom I fell down, but I knew Miss Edna wouldn't let me get by with that answer.

"Gorilla George gave it to me."

She looked at me a little longer and asked why I called him that name. I told her he was as big as a gorilla and probably just about as smart as one too.

"What did you do to make him do that to you?"

I told her, "Miss Edna, I didn't have to do anything to him; he just does it because he can."

Miss Edna said, "No, child, he does it because nobody stops him."

I assured her I was not the one who could stop him. I told her I was not the only one he bullied.

She called her husband, "Edgar! Edgar! Please come here!"

Mr. Williams was a big man. He never said much to me when I came over to visit. When he walked in the room, she said, "Edgar, look at that child's eye!"

"What do you want me to do about it, woman?"

"I want you to teach him how to defend himself." I found out Mr. Williams had been a boxer in his younger days.

Even though I tried to get out of a boxing lesson, Miss Edna wouldn't hear of it. She said, "Child, I don't want you to learn to go beat up people, but I do want you to learn to defend yourself. My Edgar can help you."

Every day for a couple of weeks, Mr. Williams worked with me. I was a fast learner.

Even though I had learned a lot, I was still scared at the prospect of trying it out on Gorilla George. What was funny was that I used my new skills on a day that George was bullying someone else.

We were on the playground, and I saw him hitting a little guy smaller than me. Even though I was scared, seeing someone mistreated made me madder than when he did it to me.

I could almost hear my heart beat as I walked over to George. He turned around, looked at me, and said, "What are you looking at, runt?"

I said, "George, leave him alone; he's not bothering you."

Mr. Williams had taught me that the most important lick in a fight was the first one. He told me to make sure I landed it hard and in a good location—preferably the nose. My heartbeat got louder and stronger as George took a swing. I ducked and landed a fist right on his nose. He started crying louder than any girl I had ever heard squeal.

I couldn't wait to tell Mr. and Mrs. Williams about my episode. Mr. Williams smiled real big when I told him.

Miss Edna said, "Child, don't you ever go around looking for trouble. Trouble has a way of finding us without any help. But don't ever stand by when someone needs you. You did good, child."

The next Sunday, I asked the young lady to stay for just a moment as she was about to leave the morning service. After everyone left, I asked her if she would trust me to help her. Again, tears came to her eyes.

"Please, Pastor, please don't go to the police!"

I told her I had no intention of going to the police. I asked if she would allow me to talk with her husband. She told me she was afraid he might hit me and hurt me like he had hurt her. I assured her I was willing to take the risk. Reluctantly, she gave me permission to talk with her husband.

The first few times I went by their house, his truck was not outside, so I didn't stop. Finally, I saw his truck parked in the front yard. I walked up to the door to knock, but I never had the chance; he met me at the door. He seemed calm when he asked, "What you want, Preacher?" I asked if I could sit down and talk with him, and he pointed to the chair.

At first, I tried some small talk to lead into the conversation, but he interrupted me and said, "You didn't come here to talk about those things, Preacher. What you want?"

"Sir," I said to him, "I am concerned a man your size would hit a lady the size of your wife."

His whole demeanor changed with that statement. He ranted and raved and told me it wasn't any of my business. If I didn't get out of his house, he threatened, he would be more than glad to throw me out. I left without saying much more.

That night, after we put our kids to bed, my wife and I had the opportunity to talk. Things get busy for a pastor; you have to take advantage of every moment you can spend with your family uninterrupted. As I looked at her and thought about how much I loved her, I couldn't imagine how a man could hurt someone so special. I also thought about Miss Edna's words: "Don't ever stand by when someone needs you."

I went into the bedroom and paced back and forth. I did everything I could to take my mind off of the situation, but it didn't work. I went to the closet to go ahead and put my clothes out for the next day when a bag fell from the top of the closet. I opened it up and saw my old wrestling tights and mask. I also had a new set of tights and a mask completely white in color. I was planning to use the new outfit and change my wrestling name, but I never had the opportunity.

No one would recognize this outfit. My heart beat a little faster as I wondered if I was about to do what my heart was telling me to do— what my mind was fighting hard to keep me from doing.

Why not? No one knew who I was when I was wrestling under a mask as The Gladiator. Why not put the tights back on and take care of some things that needed to be righted?

I took my wrestling boots from the bottom of the closet and put them in the bag. As I walked through the living room, I told my wife I had to go to the office and take care of a few things. I told her I'd be back shortly.

I went to a local gas station that had a restroom located outside, away from the pumps. I put on my tights and boots and put my sweats on over them. I wouldn't put the mask on until it was time to deal with the wife beater. Then, I went to the local watering hole that I knew he frequented.

I was in luck when I got to the bar; his truck was parked on the side, and I saw him talking to someone as he was making his way to his truck. I quickly parked in a secluded place and took off the sweats and put on the mask.

As he walked toward his truck, I stepped out of the darkness and asked, "Excuse me, sir, could you tell me where the local meeting of the wife-beaters' club is?"

He smirked and said, "You're a little early for Halloween, aren't you?"

I said, "I'll get right to the point, sir. I love this town and the people in it. I keep my ear to the ground, and I hear about some rotten things that people do—like hitting a small, defenseless woman. I've heard about you. If you ever hit your wife again, I want you to know I'll be coming to see you. I'll see how you do against someone your own size."

Now at this point, I have to stop and tell you something. Ministers don't get to work off the stress and frustration they face. Most of the time, they keep it bottled inside. I was at my breaking point. I had been out of wrestling for a few months and had not worked off any of my frustration like I could when I was in the ring. I was actually looking forward to working off my stress.

I couldn't have planned it better. He took a swing at me. I grabbed his arm and gave him an arm-drag take down. It felt great. I heard the wind leave his lungs when he hit the ground. He wasn't too bright; he got up for more. It felt great body slamming someone again. I bounced him around like a rag doll.

As he lay on the ground, I kneeled down and said, "Now remember, if it ever gets back to me that you've been hitting your wife again, I'll be back for round two! I am The Masked Saint, and I'm not going to let injustices like this happen anymore."

He wasn't in any condition to follow me. I was able to get away, make my way back to the gas station, and change. When I arrived home, my wife was waiting and didn't seem to suspect a thing.

The next day, I looked in the paper and found an obscure little story in the local section entitled, "Masked Man Beats Up Local Man."

The way he told the story, he was the victim. It didn't matter to me, though. I did something instead of sitting back and letting an injustice continue. I got excited about the prospect of being able to help people who were being mistreated. The Masked Saint could help those who couldn't help themselves.

CHAPTER SIX

THE HYPOCRITE

Webster defines a hypocrite as "a person who pretends to be what he is not." The truth is, you find them everywhere. In my lifetime, I have found grocery store owners who were hypocrites. That discovery didn't stop me from buying groceries. I have found car dealers who were hypocrites. That didn't stop me from buying cars. Hypocrite lawyers—I don't even have to go there. But the most despicable hypocrite is the one found in the church. And every church has its hypocrite(s).

Our hypocrite's name was Judd (his God-given name was Justice, but everyone called him Judd). Judd owned a local business and was very successful. You would see him in church every time the doors were open.

I first learned about him when I had an opportunity to visit the folks who visited our church. They would always say, "Does that guy who owns the store downtown belong to your church?"

"Are you talking about Judd? Yes, he's a member." Those folks usually didn't show back up at church anymore.

I always went to see Judd after an incident like that. When I shared what people were saying, he would get mad and blame everyone else but himself.

Then, when we had our quarterly business meeting, Judd would get very irritated if something didn't go his way. He always came to me and explained what I "should have done."

More and more, I found out why Judd was frowned on by so many people. I thought, *Why, Lord? Why me? Of all the churches in the county, why does the biggest hypocrite in the county have to belong to the church I pastor?*

The day before our next business meeting, I was sitting at my desk, trying to think about the business that would come up at the meeting the next day. I could see there were some potential "hot" items, sure to make Judd unhappy. As I often did, I thought back to Miss Edna and the lessons I learned from her.

I remembered the time I told her about an incident that happened in school. I had run for class president and didn't win. The guy who did win acted one way at church and a different way at school.

Since most of the people in my town went to the same church, most of our school's teachers went to that church. They all knew him. They just didn't know what he was like when he wasn't around adults or kids in his clique. I knew, though. I knew how he treated kids he didn't like.

While talking to Miss Edna about my heartache, I said, "I'm not gonna go back to that church anymore!"

Miss Edna had a way of making sense out of things that didn't make sense. She smiled and said, "Why are you not going back to church, child?"

I felt strong in my answer this time: "Because it's full of hypocrites!"

"Think about what you just said, child. Is the church really 'full' of hypocrites?"

"No, ma'am, I guess it ain't full of 'em, but he's in there, and I ain't going back!"

When Miss Edna rolled her eyes, I knew she wasn't too thrilled with my answers. She was so gentle and loving. She always seemed to know the right thing to say.

"Listen to me, child. As long as you live, you're going to run into hypocrites! You have the option of letting the hypocrite stop you from going to church, but if you do, that means you are smaller than the hypocrite."

"I don't understand, Miss Edna," I said with a sigh.

"Well, child, anything you hide behind has got to be bigger than you are. If you hide behind a hypocrite and let him keep you away from church, then he's bigger than you are."

Suddenly the phone rang and stopped my daydream of the past. It was another one of my members who was also concerned about the upcoming business meeting. He went on and on about how Judd's attitude was hurting the witness of our church. I assured him I would try to do a better job of moderating the meeting.

I must admit, I did have a few knots in my stomach as I started the meeting the next night. And just as I had thought, Judd made everyone miserable with his rants and the way he conducted himself.

When people didn't vote the way he thought they should vote, Judd blamed me. After the meeting, he stuck his finger in my face and went on and on about what he thought should have been done. I didn't sleep very well that night.

By Saturday, I was able to stop thinking about it so much. That was the day of the church league softball game. I loved playing softball. Our team wasn't the best team, but we usually won our fair share of games.

I always picked up an old deacon named Bob to take him to the game. He didn't play, but he would watch, and then after the game, I would take him to the local Pizza Hut. His wife had died the year before, and he was lonely, with no other family around. He was a good man, and I always enjoyed spending time with him. We always invited him over to spend the holidays with our family. He looked forward to Saturdays also.

On this day, we were tied going into the bottom of the ninth inning. All we needed was one more out, and we would go into extra innings. The ball was hit to Judd. Judd missed the mark on his throw and the guy was able to score, ending the game. Oh, well, it was still a good game, and in fifty years, no one would remember that we had lost.

As we were walking off the field, shaking hands with the opposing team, I heard Judd running off at the mouth. He was running down the young man he had thrown the ball to and blaming everyone on the team but himself for the loss.

It was one of those times when I just snapped and said, "Judd, why don't you shut your big mouth for once?" Not only was Judd surprised, but I surprised everyone else on the team.

Judd responded by saying, "You can't tell me to shut up!"

To which I responded, "I just did. Shut your mouth, or I'll shut it for you!" I must admit, that response surprised me too when it came out of my mouth.

Judd did the wrong thing; he started running toward me. It was as if it happened in slow motion. As he got closer to me, my instincts took over, and I dropped him like a bad habit. Boom! He hit the ground. It was as if my life passed before my eyes. It was like I had an angel on one shoulder telling me, "No, no, don't do this!" But there was a devil on the other shoulder telling me, "Hit the sorry rascal!"

After I hit him, I knew my ministry was over at this church. How in the world would they let me continue on being the pastor when I had hit a member of my church?

When Judd woke up, he got up, saying, "I'm going to have you before the deacons and the church! You're gone, Pastor; you're gone!"

As Bob and I were driving back home (neither one of us felt like eating pizza after this incident), I said, "Well, Bob, it looks like I'm through as pastor of our church." Bob tried to comfort me as best as he could.

I took Bob to his house and headed to mine. My wife was working in the yard when I pulled up in the driveway. She knew something was wrong by the look on my face. "Was it a bad loss?"

"Yes, honey, I think I lost more than the game."

When I told her what I had done to Judd, she couldn't believe it. She didn't say anything, but I could tell she wanted to say a lot.

I called the chairman of deacons and told him what I had done, and I suggested calling a retired minister who was a member of our church to have him give the sermon the next day. I told him I would meet with the deacons the next afternoon and resign. I told him I would do the best job I could not to hurt the church any more than I already had.

About an hour later, the chairman called me and said, "I've talked to all the other deacons and they don't want the retired minister to preach. They want you to preach. We'll meet tomorrow afternoon and try to hash this thing out."

I couldn't believe what I heard. I told him I didn't know how in the world I could stand behind the pulpit and preach after I had hurt God's work the way I had. He stood firm in his request for me to continue on until we met.

I had such a hard time sleeping that night. I felt like the hypocrite of all hypocrites. I felt like God should strike me dead for what I had done. Things like this have a way of moving very quickly through a small community like ours. I knew everyone in the church would know about what had taken place on the softball field. I wanted to go and hide under some rock, but I couldn't. I would have to face the music.

Again, I thought about Miss Edna's words. If you stand behind the hypocrite, you're smaller than the hypocrite. I prayed and asked for God's forgiveness and His guidance.

We had two services on Sunday. I preached at eight-thirty and eleven o'clock. The eight-thirty service was usually smaller in attendance than the one at eleven. That was the service the "early risers" came to.

After the music ended, I stepped down from the pulpit area and stood on the floor in front of the people. Judd was there that morning, sneering at me from his pew.

I looked at the people and said, "I've heard about people giving God's work a 'bloody nose,' but I never thought I would be one of those people. I did something yesterday I am very ashamed of. I hit a member of this congregation on the softball field. His name is Judd Harrison, and he's sitting right over there." (He looked like a calf looking at a new gate when every head turned around to see him.)

"Judd is one of the most reprehensible human beings I have ever met, but that was no reason to do what I did. I've asked God to forgive me, and I know He has. I would also like to ask Judd to forgive me, and I would like to ask you as a congregation to forgive me."

"I couldn't get up in the pulpit this morning and be a hypocrite. I couldn't preach until you knew I had failed and am sorry. I'm just a simple human being like you. I make mistakes just like you do. Again, I'm sorry."

I thought I preached better than I had ever preached before after my confession to the congregation. But I knew I had to do the same thing over again at the eleven o'clock service.

After the service was over, the first man to come out the door hugged me (and he never hugged anyone) and whispered into my ear, "I'd have paid ten bucks to see you knock that rascal on his butt!"

Maybe I wouldn't have to resign after all.

By the time the eleven o'clock service rolled around, I think everyone who was a member showed up for service. The word had gotten around.

I did the same thing I had done before the eight-thirty service, saying much of the same thing I had said earlier. After I finished, as I walked back up to the pulpit, a member on the second row stood up and said, "I think we should stand in support of our pastor!" The whole congregation stood up and applauded.

As my wife and I drove home after the service, I said to her, "Have you ever heard of a minister who knocked a member of his church on his rear end and got a standing ovation?"

Judd didn't act the same after that event happened. He was always nice to me and other folks from that day on—and he always spoke to me from a distance.

CHAPTER SEVEN

AN UNLIKELY OCCUPATION

I t was unusual how I got into wrestling. I never sat down one day and said, "I think I'll become a professional wrestler."

My wife and I graduated from college together and moved back to my hometown. My wife got a job teaching math at the high school she graduated from. I didn't want to go right to seminary after leaving college, so I thought I would try and get some experience in the ministry as a youth minister. I was still very young and the prospects of a church calling a pastor as young as I was did not look very bright.

I put my resume out in the area and played the waiting game, hoping a church would call me to be their youth pastor.

I had taken a job working for the local Coca Cola Bottling Company while I waited for a church to contact me. I had a lot of spare time to work out in the gym. I loved lifting weights and working out. I was in great shape.

As I was looking at the *Tampa Tribune*, I saw an ad that caught my eye: Wanted: Professional Wrestlers. My wife was not too thrilled when I showed her the ad. And she surely wasn't too thrilled to see my excitement over the ad.

"Come on, honey. What have I got to lose?" It didn't take her long to tell me.

"You could get a broken arm or leg or head. Have you seen how those guys get tossed around? You could get hurt badly."

I assured her that I would just go down and check it out. I promised I wouldn't do anything without first running it by her. Even though she didn't look convinced, she knew I was going to do it.

I made sure I put on a pair of shorts, T-shirt, and gym shoes before I made my way to Tampa. I was going to be prepared—just in case I could start training that night.

As I drove to Tampa, I couldn't help thinking back to my childhood. If anyone had ever told me I could do something like this then, I would have said he was crazy. Like I said before, I was a very sickly child.

I had pneumonia about six times before I became a teenager. It seemed I was always sick while growing up.

The greatest scare came when I was in the fourth grade. I got up one morning feeling terrible. I didn't mention it to my mom because I knew she would make me stay at home. I felt warm all over, and my eyes felt like they were on fire.

When I got to school, I continued to feel worse and worse. When it came time for recess, I ran with my buddies out onto the playground. My legs felt rubbery as I ran, causing me to fall head first into a tetherball pole. I hit my head pretty hard, but there was no blood. After getting up, I spent the rest of the time sitting in the shade, feeling worse by the minute.

When we got back into class, I felt nauseous. When I laid my head on my desk, it prompted Mrs. Guthrie, my fourth grade teacher, to tell me to sit up straight.

I told her I wasn't feeling well, but she said I probably overdid it at recess. Before I knew it, I threw up all over my desk. I think Mrs. Guthrie finally believed me.

She felt of my forehead and said, "Chris, you are burning up. Go down to the office and tell them what happened."

It didn't take long before they called my mom. When she picked me up, she took me straight to the doctor's office. Within a short period of time, I was being admitted to the Winter Haven Hospital.

I had the greatest doctor anyone could ever ask for. His name was Dr. Raymond LaRue. He was one of the most caring men I have ever met.

That evening, Dr. LaRue came into my room and asked my mom to take a seat. He pulled a chair up close to her and said, "Chris is a very sick little boy. He has a bad concussion, but that's the least of his problems."

The concussion had obviously occurred when I hit my head on the tetherball pole.

"Chris also has viral encephalitis and polio."

Even though my mom didn't know what those diseases were, she knew it wasn't good. Dr. LaRue comforted my mom as she cried.

"Will he be all right, Dr. LaRue?"

"I'm going to do all I can, but ultimately, he is in God's hands."

I slept a lot during the early part of my illness. Sometimes I seemed to be in a weird state of mind. My eyes were closed, but I could hear what was going on around me. There were many times I heard my mother cry and pray for my recovery. I could hear my mom and dad's voices, but I couldn't respond.

One night while I was in that condition, I felt a hand on mine. I could tell it was Miss Edna because she sang and hummed a lot. She rubbed my hand and was humming "Amazing Grace."

After she got through humming and singing, I heard her pray: "Dear Lord, this is a precious child here. He ain't been here long enough to do what You got for him to do. I know he's going to be all right. Please be with his folks, and give them strength during this time. Thank You, Lord, for being so good to us. Amen."

It was such a simple prayer, but it was one of those moments when I knew I was going to be okay. Miss Edna had a way of lifting me up like no other person.

I was in the hospital for over three months. I don't think my folks ended up paying my entire hospital bill until I was in high school. My recovery was a long process, but ultimately, I made it through that difficult time.

The funny thing was that late at night about the only thing on TV was professional wrestling. I found myself watching wrestling every opportunity I could. I got hooked.

Wrestling was great in those days. It was good against evil. The good guys usually prevailed. You didn't see any of the stuff you see today in wrestling.

Dr. LaRue would not allow me to give up. Even after I got out of the hospital, he made me swim and walk and learn to lift weights. He was the reason I became such a gym rat.

I was a little nervous as I entered the gym. There were several guys who had answered the ad. But I looked to be in better shape than most of them.

Suddenly a guy stepped out of the office and called all of us over to where he was standing. I couldn't believe it. There was the Great Malenko. I remembered great matches between him and Eddie Graham.

I had grown up watching him. He was the perennial bad guy. It was he who had placed the ad in the paper. He was the one who taught me to wrestle. It is important to emphasize that he did, indeed, *teach me to wrestle.* He wanted me to be able to protect myself. He was a great teacher.

I signed up that night and even got the opportunity to get on the mat. I was hooked. I had to pay him to train me, but I was willing to do it, and it was worth every penny.

Each time I got into the ring, I enjoyed it more and more. It all seemed to come naturally for me. Six months later, I was ready for my first match.

I can remember my first match like it was yesterday. He was bigger than I was and had obviously been wrestling a lot longer than I had. My adrenaline was flowing strong. I was trying to remember everything I had been taught. Within five minutes, I had a broken nose and mat burns on my elbows and knees. But every time I got into the ring, I learned a lesson that helped me prepare for the next match.

I loved watching the fans scream and jump up and down, cheering for their favorite. I loved the smell of the arena and the atmosphere of a great crowd.

Professional wrestling wasn't something a whole lot of people wanted to do, but for me, it was some of the greatest times I have ever had. Believe it or not, it has helped me a lot in life.

CHAPTER EIGHT
THE YOUTH PASTOR

finally got a call from a church looking for a youth pastor. It was a large, county-seat church, not too far from where we lived. Fortunately, moving there didn't put my wife any farther away from the school where she taught. The sad thing was I wasn't able to continue wrestling. I would be a full-time youth pastor.

Being a youth pastor certainly didn't help our bank account. We were barely able to make ends meet, even with my wife teaching full time. But I was fulfilling the will of God for my life. Things were going along normally until my wife shared some of the greatest news I have ever heard.

One day after I arrived home and after we had eaten our evening meal, she asked me to sit on the couch with her. I could tell something was on her mind. I was trying to think of what she was going to share with me.

Would it be, "We are barely making ends meet," or "I'm not happy," or "This house is too small"? Whatever it was, I could tell it was something of great importance.

She sat on the couch and took my hand and said, "Chris, we are going to have a baby!"

I jumped to my feet and squealed like a kid. Words alone cannot fully express how my heart leaped for joy.

Then it hit me. How could we survive with a new addition to the family? After all, we were barely making ends meet with what we were both making.

After we called the future grandparents and other relatives to share the good news, my wife and I went out for a walk. We talked about names and what he or she would be like and so many other things. I certainly didn't want to throw a wet blanket on our joy, but in my mind, I was trying to figure out how we could make it financially.

The next day, I sat at my office desk and tried to think. I couldn't get a second job; the church certainly wouldn't permit that to happen. Then I thought, *I do get a couple of days off a week. I am still in good shape. Why couldn't I wrestle a couple of nights a week?*

No. The pastor of the church would never permit that to happen. But what if I wore a mask and wrestled? I honestly couldn't see a downside to the solution.

When I got home, I shared my idea with my wife. She wasn't thrilled. "What if the church finds out? They might fire you, and then we would be in worse shape."

"But honey, I'm going to wear a mask and wrestle under a different identity. No one will know. I'm not doing anything illegal or immoral. I'm just trying to help my family survive financially. I'm going to use the talent God has given me to do something to help our family. And it is something I enjoy doing. How can that be bad?"

Reluctantly, she agreed. So, I called a promoter and asked if he could use me a couple of nights a week. It was all set. I ordered a mask and trunks from the outfitter in Youngstown, Ohio. I was ready to go.

My mind wandered back to a conversation I had with Miss Edna about truth and trust. I had torn my new school clothes, and I was upset because my mom had always told me to take my school clothes off when I came home. I had climbed a tree and torn my new jeans. I was worried about telling my mom. But Miss Edna always had a way of putting things in perspective.

"Child, truth and trust are wonderful things. The Lord said the truth would set us free. Always be truthful. But sometimes you have to be careful with the truth. If someone isn't pretty, you don't have to lie and say she is. You just say something else nice about her. You can say she looks nice or smells good."

"Trust is something people don't give you, child. It's something you have to earn. Trust is something that takes time with people. Every time you cause someone to lose trust in you, you have to start all over again, building your trust back up in that person's eyes."

Tuesday was one of my days off. I would be working that night for the first time under the mask. I was excited to be back in the ring again. I got to the arena early to loosen up. I found out I would be working against Adorable Adrian Adonis. He was a big fella who had been working a long time.

In the middle of the match, he had me in the corner and was going to do a "Flying Veel." He had one hand under my right arm, up close to the shoulder, and the other hand around my neck. We took two steps forward, and he threw me into the air; I was supposed to land on my back. Unfortunately, I landed on my shoulder. It was painful. I knew I would be feeling it for a couple of days.

I made it through the match and got paid for a good night's work. Mission accomplished.

The next day, I was extremely sore. My shoulder hurt, and I had a few bumps and bruises. What would I say if the pastor or someone else at church asked me what happened?

It didn't take long for my fears to become a reality. As I walked into the office, the pastor did a double take as he looked at me. "Chris, are you all right?"

"Yes, sir, I'm fine."

"How did you get those bruises on your arm? And why are you holding your arm like that?"

"Oh, I fell last night."

That wasn't a lie; I did fall. I just didn't tell him I had a lot of help falling.

Thank God things worked out, and I was able to carry on working as a youth pastor, also working a couple of nights a week as The Gladiator. However, the church thought they had one of the world's clumsiest youth pastors. He always had bruises from "falling down."

CHAPTER NINE

THE OUTCAST

I t felt a little strange on that morning when my secretary buzzed me and told me a police detective wanted to see me. As I invited him into my office, he introduced himself to me: "Reverend Samuels, my name is Jim Harper, and I'm investigating an assault that took place outside Percy's Bar." The detective told me the name of the man who had been assaulted.

"I believe her husband said his wife is a member of your church."

"Yes, yes she is."

"To be honest with you, Reverend, I think he got what he deserved. I can't tell you how many times one of our officers has been called to his home because of a disturbance. But I have to investigate any lead that might be helpful."

This certainly didn't work out the way I thought it would. I had visions of jail and front-page stories written about me.

"Pastor, I'm trying to see if maybe she was seeing someone in the church and he beat the husband up. Have you noticed her speaking to someone pretty regularly?"

"No, sir, she's usually the last person in the church and the first one out the door. She pretty much keeps to herself."

"Well, I've done what I was supposed to do," he said as he began making his way to my door.

"The assailant told the guy he was 'The Masked Saint.' If he takes care of a few more guys like that, he'll be a saint in my book!"

Whew! Close call! I thought, as I walked him to the door.

"Reverend, I wish I could send this masked guy to visit some other folks who needed humbling."

I couldn't believe what he was saying. Did he really want someone other than an officer of the law to take justice into his own hands?

"Let me know if there is anything else I can do for you, Detective Harper."

"Thanks, Reverend, I'll do it."

When the officer left, the church secretary came into my office. I thought she was going to ask me about the detective and his visit; she seemed a little uneasy.

"What's wrong, Mrs. Read?"

"Pastor, there's a woman outside who wants to see you. She doesn't have an appointment and—," she paused.

"Yes, what is it?"

"Well, Pastor, she isn't dressed very ladylike."

"Okay, Mrs. Read, let her in."

As the woman walked into the office, I could understand what Mrs. Read meant; the woman definitely didn't look like the average church member. Her attire was a little risqué. I invited her in and asked her to take a seat.

She said, "My name is Valerie, and I really appreciate you taking time to see me."

"It's my pleasure, ma'am. What can I do to help?"

I could tell she was carrying a big burden. I've seen the look so many times on the faces of people who are hurting. Her stare was kind of hollow. She didn't look me in the eye; she looked to the side as she tried to verbalize what was on the inside.

Her chin trembled as she spoke, "Reverend, I'm at the end of my rope, and I don't know what to do. I didn't know where else to go. When I was a little girl, we used to attend a church that looked like this one. I've passed this church every day since I came to town."

She told me where she lived, and I knew it was a rough section of town. She told me a story I've heard before about a life that took some wrong turns and finally went into a tailspin. She told me she had ended up on the street and was a prostitute.

"Can you help me get out of this lifestyle, Reverend?"

Of all the times I had talked to people in her condition, no one had ever asked me that question. On the one hand, I was thrilled that she wanted to get out of that lifestyle, but on the other hand, I knew it would be a difficult journey.

I asked her if she had any education. She not only had graduated from high school, but she had also attended community college for a couple of years. I told her I would begin immediately trying to help her find employment.

She looked down at the carpet and then looked up and said, "Reverend, I don't have much money; most of the money I made was taken from me."

The money was taken by her pimp. Not only did he keep her continually needing his assistance, but he also was abusive and she was very afraid of him. She had tried before to get out of prostitution, but he had abused her even more for trying. I was literally her last hope of ever getting out of this type of life.

I told her I would do all I could to help her. The first thing I had to do was find another place for her to live. Our church was a financial supporter of the local women's shelter, and I felt sure I could get her in if they had room. I called the director of the shelter and found out there was one room available.

I also wanted her to find some new friends, so I invited her to church. She hesitated at the thought of coming to church. How would people receive her? I assured her that she would be welcomed. Little did I know inviting her to church would create a problem.

I also began trying to find her a job. I was sure, with the education she had, we would be able to find her something quickly.

The next Sunday, Valerie walked into the service several minutes after the first song. She sat on the very back row. She looked down at the floor, very seldom looking up.

Then, a terrible thing happened. It seemed that every eye in the building began turning back to look at the latecomer. It was almost like she could feel all eyes looking back at her.

I raised my voice a couple of octaves, trying to get folks to look forward, without much success. As soon as the closing prayer was over, she made her way out of the building very quickly.

I noticed people standing in groups talking. Some were pointing to the pew she had been sitting in. I wasn't surprised when a couple of the deacons asked to speak with me in my office before I left. I knew what the conversation would be about.

As we walked into the office, one of the men began speaking before I could even shut the door. "Pastor, we can't have a woman like that coming to our church," he said with smugness.

The other man didn't say anything. He just nodded in agreement with everything his friend had to say.

"Oh," I said, "and exactly what kind of a woman is she?" He was so rattled, he stuttered as he tried to express his point.

"You know what I mean, Reverend."

Not only did my heart hurt to hear one of my members saying something like this, it also enraged me. "Sir," I said, trying to make eye contact with him, "you need to read your Bible and remember how the Lord treated people who didn't come from the best of backgrounds."

As I brought up passage after passage, my mind wandered back to an incident that happened when I was a boy.

I remembered a day I couldn't wait to get to Miss Edna's after school. She usually made a big ol' apple pie on Sunday afternoons; since this was Monday, I was sure she would have some left. No one made apple pie like Miss Edna. As luck would have it, the first thing she asked me after I came into the house was if I wanted a big slice of apple pie.

After I had my pie, Miss Edna always wanted to know how my day at school had gone. After I shared the highlights of the day, I told her a young woman had moved into our neighborhood. I asked if she had met her, but she didn't even know someone new had come to town. The word had gotten around pretty quickly that the young woman was also a mother and no one had seen a man at the house.

Miss Edna grew irritated very quickly and told me I should never jump to conclusions about people. She also asked why I hadn't gone over to welcome her to the neighborhood. I told her my mom wouldn't let me get near her house.

Miss Edna went into a long story about how we should treat people the way we would want to be treated. "That's the Golden Rule, child. You should've heard me talk about that as many times as you've been in my house." I thanked her for the pie and left.

The next Sunday at church was a real humdinger. The woman from our neighborhood showed up. No one talked to her—not even the preacher. She and her little girl sat on the back row all alone. After the service was over, they walked out without anyone saying a word. I could see some of the men going up to the preacher and talking as they pointed to the woman and her child getting into their car.

I couldn't wait to get to Miss Edna's the next day after school. Not only was I looking forward to a big piece of apple pie, but I also wanted to tell her about what had gone on at church.

Miss Edna said, "Her name is Marsha, and her little girl's name is Megan."

I asked how she knew that. Miss Edna had gone over the very day I told her a new person had moved into the neighborhood.

Miss Edna seemed to be a little disappointed in me that I had not tried to make friends with her little girl. I told her again that my mom had told me not to go over there. Miss Edna just stared out her window and said, "I know how she feels, child. I know how she feels."

As I left her house, I walked slowly by the house of the newcomers. I stood in front of the house and looked for any sign of life. I looked over at Miss Edna's house and looked back at the house. All of a sudden, the woman said, "Hello! What's your name?"

I told her my name and started walking towards her house. The little girl came out of the house and hid behind her mother. All of a sudden, I heard my mother calling my name in the tone that meant I better get moving. I told them bye as I made my way back to my house.

My mom wasn't too happy with me when I walked in the door. "Didn't I tell you not to go over to that house? Didn't I tell you not to talk with those people?" I just stood there, looking down at the ground as she continued to reprimand me.

Later that night, before I went to bed, I asked my mom if I could talk with her. She came into my room and sat on my bed next to me. "What is it, honey?"

"Mom, why can't I talk with that lady?"

She seemed irritated and said, "Because I told you not to, and that's the end of it. Now go to sleep."

Before she turned off the light, I asked her, "Mom, how would you want people to treat you if you were that woman?" She didn't answer me, but I could tell my question went straight to her heart.

As I came home from school the next day, I couldn't believe my eyes. My mom was standing in the yard, talking to the woman she had told me not to talk with. As I walked closer, she called for me to come to her. She said, "Honey, this is Miss Marsha. Her daughter's name is Megan. Why don't you invite her to come over sometime?"

I was shocked, but I was also very glad. My mom befriended that lady and also talked to the folks at church about doing the right thing. Miss Edna was always the one who seemed to get the right thing started in our neighborhood.

I could see the conversation wasn't going very well with the deacons, but I was driven to help them see what should be done. I would work on this one a little at a time. My next order of business was to make sure Valerie's pimp left her alone.

Later that night, I got my tights, boots, and mask and went downtown. I parked my car at a large store parking lot.

I waited in the alley behind a dumpster located close to where the pimp was known to "encourage" his women. I had Valerie in a safe place, but I knew he would not leave her alone.

A couple of the women came into the alley, and I saw the pimp arguing with them about money. He slapped one forcefully across the face. The women made their way to the street while he went to the pay phone and called someone. This was my opportunity.

As I walked up behind him, he turned around and saw me. He slowly hung up the phone and smiled as he lit a cigarette. "What you dressed up for, dude? This ain't Halloween."

"I'm here to tell you that you are officially out of business."

"Say what?" he said laughingly.

"From this point on, you will find another line of work in another location."

He continued to halfway laugh as he sized me up. "What you gonna do if I decide I like my work and location?"

"Well, I guess I'll just have to change your mind."

He reached in his pocket and pulled out a knife and said, "Well, I'm just gonna show you who is in charge, homeboy," as he started toward me.

I grabbed the wrist of his knife hand and threw him into the building like I was throwing someone into the ropes in the ring. The knife fell out of his hand as he staggered back towards me. I picked him up and body slammed him to the ground. I could hear the wind leave his lungs as he landed, obviously in pain.

I knelt down and said, "You listen to me and listen real good. If I ever see you here on these streets again, I will come back. This little match is nothing compared to what you will receive the next time I come. Do you understand me?"

He nodded slightly, still trying to get the wind back in his lungs. "When you get up from here, you tell those other women that you are officially turning over a new leaf and they need to find other employment. Do you understand that?" This time he nodded a little more convincingly.

I made my way back down the alley and put my sweats back on and made my way to the car. I felt this problem was taken care of, but the one left with the deacons would be a bigger battle.

I asked God to grant me wisdom. He seemed to remind me about Miss Edna and my mom treating people the way they would want to be treated. Then I remembered the Scripture passage about Jesus dealing with a woman who had been caught in the very act of adultery.

In that day, the woman could have been stoned. When they brought the woman to Jesus and told Him what Moses said to do to her, they asked Him, "What do you say we should do to her?" The Scripture says that Jesus knelt down and started writing in the dirt. One commentator suggests that Jesus was writing down the sins of those who were accusing the woman. That was the answer.

I hadn't been a pastor very long, but I knew I had heard some things about a few of my deacons from people who were not members. I preached about hypocrisy, hoping they would get the message. They obviously had not gotten the message.

I invited the deacons into my office and told them we needed to meet about Valerie coming to our church. They came in and sat down, and I stood at a little blackboard. I told them the story about Jesus and the woman found in the very act of adultery. I told them about Him stooping down to write on the ground and that He was probably writing the sins of those standing around Him.

"Gentlemen, I haven't been here very long, but I have been here long enough to have several people tell me about some men in our church who live one way in the church and a different way when they leave."

I turned around and wrote several words on the blackboard: *Deceit;* I knew one of them bragged about cheating on his taxes, and I looked him in the eye. *Dishonesty;* I knew one of the men overcharged the city for repairs he did on their cars, and I looked him in the eye. *Drunkenness;* I had seen one of the men coming out of the local watering hole several times, and I looked him in the eye.

They all looked down at the floor. "Gentlemen, Jesus forgave the woman who was caught in the act of adultery and told her 'to go and not make sin a way of life.'"

They gradually looked at me, and I said, "Gentlemen, we are going to do the right thing and treat this woman like we would want to be treated if we had made mistakes in our lives. Do you understand me?" There wasn't much said as they made their way out of the office.

Valerie was a life that was saved. She changed her lifestyle, got a good job, and amazingly made friends with people who once had treated her like an outcast.

CHAPTER TEN
THE MISTAKE

I don't think I have ever done anything more stressful than being the pastor of a church. You have to preach every week. Even when you get a vacation, you're thinking about the next sermon when you get back. You deal with a lot of heartache. You walk with people through death and other crises. You carry the weight of a lot of people's burdens. You get calls at all hours of the night and morning.

It feels good to get away for a little while. When you have the opportunity to attend any type of conference that will help you to serve better, you take it.

I had been working a lot of hours. I had dealt with a lot of hurts over the past few weeks. I felt like I had neglected my family quite a bit. But there was a light at the end of the tunnel. I was going to attend a conference in West Palm Beach. My girls were out of school, and they would be able to attend with me.

We were all excited. We would leave after the service on Sunday and travel to South Florida to the conference. I had made friends with a pastor in the next community. He had two boys the same age as my daughters. His wife was a teacher, just like my wife. They were also going to attend the conference. We were planning to stay in the same hotel. Pastor Ron and I would attend the conference, and our families could visit the beach and visit some of the other local sites. We were all so excited.

Unfortunately, sometimes things don't go the way we had hoped. An older member of our church passed away, and I would have to perform the funeral on Monday morning. My girls were very disappointed.

I asked my pastor friend if my girls could ride with them on Sunday and go ahead and check into the hotel. I would leave immediately after the funeral and meet them later that afternoon. Even though my family was happy with the idea, my stress level increased. Everything was set.

Instead of driving with my family on Sunday afternoon, I was preparing a funeral sermon. It took a lot for me to concentrate, but I finally finished the funeral message. I went to the home of the family whose family member had passed away and tried to minister to them. It went well.

That night I packed my bag and was ready to leave after the funeral the next day. Hopefully, nothing would keep me from my new plans. I called the girls to make sure they had arrived and were having a good time. My wife said the girls were very excited.

The funeral went as well as could be expected, and I left for the conference. I could finally breathe a sigh of relief. For the next couple of days, I would be able to "chill out."

As I was driving down the turnpike, my stomach rumbled. I hadn't eaten breakfast or lunch, and I was very hungry. The only thing on the turnpike is fast food, but it would do in a pinch.

As I walked up to front of the service plaza, three large young hoods forced their way in front of me as I tried to open the door. *Patience, Chris, patience*, I said to myself.

I went to the restroom to wash my face and hands. That would give me a moment to let my heart rate go down. Being in the ministry, I didn't get to relieve my stress like I did when I was wrestling regularly. And with the stress load I was under, I needed to calm down.

When I went into the fast-food restaurant, those same three hoods butted in front of me as I went up to give my order. Again, I said to myself, *Patience, patience!*

I gave my order, and the young lady who waited on me gave me a cup for my drink. As I started over to drink machine—you guessed it—those same three hoods butted in front of me again. Enough was enough. I couldn't contain myself any longer.

"Hey, guys, you need to go to the back of the line and wait your turn like everyone else."

The people around me had evidently also experienced their rude behavior and were very glad someone had the nerve to speak up. What took place next happened very quickly, yet in my mind, it felt like it was in slow motion.

One of the hoods looked me in the eye and used a vulgar word and a vulgar sign right in my face. My stress load had reached its limit. I hit him so hard it lifted him off his feet. I put an elbow in the chest of the one to my left. I could hear the air leave his lungs. As the third one swung at me, I ducked and put my foot right on his knee. He wouldn't be walking for a long time.

Just like that, it was over. People were running in all directions. The manager was on the radio, calling for help.

The Florida State Troopers are in charge of security at the service plazas on the turnpike. The trooper was there in a matter of minutes, and before long, I was wearing handcuffs and sitting in a lonely room in the service plaza.

My mind was going a thousand miles per hour. My ministry would be over. I was probably going to be on the local TV stations. I might even make national news. It would be very embarrassing to the church I served. And I couldn't even think of all the things my wife would say to me.

As I sat there handcuffed, waiting for the state trooper to take me away, I couldn't help but think back to one of my visits with Miss Edna. She had more patience and grace than anyone I have ever known. She had talked to me many times about my temper. She talked to me many times about thinking before I acted.

As I walked up her driveway on one particular day, there was a police car in front of her house. The policeman was just getting in his car to leave. I ran to her front door, calling her name loudly as I approached: "Miss Edna, Miss Edna, are you all right?"

She came to door smiling, like every other time I had knocked on her door. "I'm fine, child. Ain't nothing wrong with me."

I asked her why the policeman was there and if everything was okay.

While she and her husband were out shopping, someone had broken into their barn and stolen some of Mr. Williams' tools. The intruder had also broken a window.

"Aren't you mad? Wouldn't you like to do something to whoever did these bad things?" Miss Edna just smiled and shook her head in the negative.

"Child, 'things' can be replaced. 'Things' ain't worth worrying yourself with."

I still couldn't understand how she could feel that way. "Oh, child, I don't like it, and I hope they catch whoever did these bad things, but I'm just glad me and Edgar weren't here while it happened. I'm glad it was only 'things' taken and broken. We are safe."

"Child, don't let little things make your stomach turn into knots. There are way too many more important things to be upset over. You can tell the size of a person by the things that get him down."

I could have walked away from those hoods. Was it really worth the possibility of losing so much? Was this a big thing to be upset over? The only thing I could think of was wishing I could have another chance to react.

As the state trooper walked into the room, I stood to my feet. Much to my surprise, he walked behind me and unlocked the handcuffs. No one was more surprised than me when he said, "Sir, you are free to go. I can't find those hoods you worked over. Sometimes it happens like this. They probably had some outstanding warrants against them. They were more worried about being put in jail than what you did to them. The manager of the restaurant doesn't want to press charges either. Frankly, I think he was happy somebody put those punks in their place. So, make sure you don't let your temper get the best of you anymore."

I felt so relieved, but I also felt guilty. I remembered Miss Edna's words, "You can always tell the size of a person by what gets him down." They were just words. I could have walked away, but I made the wrong choice. Fortunately, it worked out for me. I had learned a great lesson.

CHAPTER ELEVEN
PREJUDICE

The sixties were volatile years. This was only a few years after Rosa Parks had refused to give up her seat on the bus in Alabama. My folks were born in South Alabama. I have learned that prejudice is something learned. My dad grew up with prejudice. Most of what I had heard about black folks was never positive. The longer I knew Mr. and Mrs. Williams, the more my prejudice went away. Miss Edna was very influential in helping me to find the call of God on my life. My dad wasn't a bad man by any means, but he was a product of what he grew up with, namely prejudice.

People can become prejudiced about many things, but when we think of the word *prejudice*, we usually associate it with skin color. I never thought I would be dealing with it in 1988, but I was wrong.

The church I pastored was a small, Southern church. The town the church was located in was divided. The community was made up of

52 percent black and 48 percent white. Little did I know when I went to pastor my first church out of seminary that a former Klansman was a member of the church. I found out while my family and I were in the receiving line, being welcomed as the new pastor. Someone came up to me and pointed out a man and said, "Do you know who that man is, Pastor?"

I assured him I knew very few people since this was my first Sunday. He said, "That's Jimmy Earl Smith. He used to be the grand dragon of the KKK."

I remember the sick feeling in the pit of my stomach as I hung my head and thought, *Why me, Lord?* I had a lot of questions come to mind as I stood there. One question was obviously answered: why there were no black people in the church.

Why was this guy a member of a church if he was that evil? Why did the members of the church let him in if they knew what he was involved in? Then, I had a thought; maybe God had gotten ahold of his heart and changed him. It didn't take long after my first conversation with him to learn that God, indeed, had not changed his heart.

I remembered a great lesson about prejudice that I learned from Miss Edna. We experienced a bad freeze one winter that affected the citrus crop throughout the state of Florida. My dad drove a truck for the citrus industry, and his work was cut back considerably. My folks were behind on their bills and things were very tight financially. My mom always planted a little garden every year, and unfortunately, the freeze also affected the garden. We were not able to enjoy the vegetables we usually had every year from the garden.

Whenever my dad became stressed, he was not very pleasant to live with. His temper was volatile and sudden when he was under stress. Not being able to pay your bills and buy groceries will stress a person out.

One afternoon while visiting with Miss Edna, she noticed I was quieter than normal. She was always so observant of my moods. "Child, why are you so quiet today?"

Even though I didn't want to tell her about my parents' troubles, I couldn't help myself. It came out of my mouth before I knew it.

"Child, are you and your family eating regularly?" I told her we were eating beans most every meal, and the servings were getting smaller and smaller.

Miss Edna said, "Child, me and Edgar have got plenty of food. Edgar has always been so smart with his gardening. Our pantry can't hold no more food. Our root cellar is full. I think I'm going to go over and take some of this food to your mama and daddy."

She looked shocked when I blurted out, "Please, Miss Edna, don't do that!"

In the short time I had been friends with Miss Edna, I never told my folks I had been going by every day to visit with her. I knew my dad wouldn't like it. I wasn't ashamed of my friendship, but as a small boy, I just didn't want to deal with my dad. And I didn't want my best friend in the world to be hurt by something my dad might say.

"Miss Edna, my dad wouldn't like it!" It didn't take very much for Miss Edna to see right through me.

"Why wouldn't he like it, child?"

"My dad doesn't talk about black folks very nice."

"Ohhh," she said, "you've never told your folks you come over here and talk to me?"

"No ma'am," I said as I hung my head.

"Don't you worry about Edna, child. But I am going over to see your folks. And I don't even need Edgar to go along with me."

I didn't know what to think after she told me what she was going to do. But I knew I was going to go with her. "I'll introduce you to my folks, Miss Edna. But if my dad says something bad to you, will you still love me and let me come over here every day?"

She had the expression of an angel on her face. She pulled me into her arms and hugged me tightly and said, "Child, I try to love like God loves us: unconditionally."

I had to ask, "What does unconditional mean?"

She said, "It means we love even when we don't get loved back."

Miss Edna asked me to bring my wagon around to the back door so we didn't have to carry all the food by arm. My heart was beating awfully fast as I opened the door of our house. "Mama, Papa, can you come here?" I asked from the front door. Miss Edna and I stood at the door as we waited for them.

I could tell when my dad saw Miss Edna that he wasn't happy. "Mama, Papa, this is my friend Miss Edna. She lives in the house way down at the end of the street. I've been going over to visit with her and Mr. Williams ever since we moved here."

Thank God at least my mother smiled and said hello. I had no idea what my dad would say.

Miss Edna didn't wait for either one of them to say anything. She just started in, "We have been so blessed by God in our garden that I wanted to share some of those blessings with you."

My dad finally spoke, "We don't need your food, and you can keep it on that wagon while you leave."

My heart sunk as I heard him insult my best friend in the whole world. I just hung my head. Miss Edna wasn't intimidated one bit. She never lost the smile on her face.

"Mr. Samuels, I have grown to love this little boy of yours like he was my own. God never seen fit to bless me with young'uns. It sure has been a joy getting to know this child."

"Well, he won't be going back over to see you anymore. I can tell you that!" my dad said as he moved closer to the door. Again, Miss Edna was not intimidated one bit.

"Mr. Samuels, may I ask you a question?" she asked, still smiling. "Do you not want my food because the food is bad, or is it because the person bringing the food is black?"

I haven't seen my dad tongue-tied too often, but this was one of those moments.

"Mr. Samuels, I can tell you are a good man. The way I know that is because I know this precious little boy of yours. Children learn the way they are from their parents. You and Mrs. Samuels have sure done a fine job raising this little boy."

"Let me tell you what I see, Mr. Samuels. I see a family that I don't know personally, outside of Chris, but I love this family 'cause that's what God would have me do. I don't see your skin color. I just see folks. It would mean a lot to me and Edgar if you would accept my gift."

My dad became a different man from that day forward. My mom fell in love with Miss Edna from that moment on. My whole family learned a great lesson.

We had a man in our church who owned a bookstore. He was from Charlotte, Michigan. He had been a funeral director and decided to sell his business and open a Hallmark store. He really was a great person.

One morning after Sunday school, he came up to me, very upset. He said, "Pastor, you know I love God and I love people. I always talk to the people who come in my store. I have a wonderful black family who comes to my store regularly. They are good, Christian people. I told them where I went to church. Pastor, they just pulled up in the parking lot. What am I going to do if someone offends them?"

It actually kind of excited me that this family had decided to come on this morning. I assumed God was ready to teach us all a lesson.

I quickly made my way to the front of the church and asked all of the ushers to meet with me.

"Guys, there is a black family in our parking lot who are about to come into our church. I wanted to chat with you a moment before they come in because I know how some of you feel about folks who don't have the same color of skin as you do."

"Let me share something with you that may help you decide how you welcome them this morning. If you do anything to hurt their feelings or turn them away, I can guarantee you that we will be on every TV station around. We might even make national news. And next week there will probably be around ten thousand people at our service to protest. I hope that helps you."

I could see the "deer in the headlights" look on their faces. But they did the right thing. They welcomed them and sat them on the front row. It was obviously time for our church to turn the corner.

I didn't know how some of the folks who had the Klansman background would respond, but I didn't care. I would be more than willing to deal with them in a different venue.

There are always people who seem to know everything in the church. I had a couple of those folks whom I had learned to love and trust. I asked them if they knew if Jimmy Earl and his friends ever met regularly—"if you know what I mean." They told me what time and where.

I decided I would scope it out first to see what I was up against. The place was way back in the woods and very secluded. That would definitely work in my favor. So, I made my way to their meeting place.

There weren't very many of them, only four or five. I could hear them talking about the visitors we had on Sunday and how they didn't like it.

"If we let that preacher get away with this, they'll be more of 'em coming, boys. We need to do something."

I decided to go back to my car and change. I couldn't wait for another night; I needed to do something tonight. I quickly changed and made my way back to their meeting place. They looked like they had seen a ghost when I stepped out of the bushes.

"Hey, guys, I think I like my costume a lot better than yours. What do you think?"

"Who in the name of Sam Hill do you think you are?"

I could see they immediately sized me up and made some looks to each other, motioning toward some tree limbs nearby.

"Hey, Jimmy, this must be the guy we've been reading about in the paper."

Jimmy Earl finally spoke. "What do you want, masked man?"

"I want you to reconsider what you are planning to do. As a matter of fact, why don't you find another church?" (Boy, I've always wanted to say that to some folks, but I've never been able to do it.)

"And if we don't, what are you going to do about it?"

"Why don't we have a meeting about it, and if I win, you stay away. No, even if I don't win, you're not going to mess with that preacher or the church."

The first guy came running at me with a stick. It was too easy. I just bent down and flipped him over. I could hear the breath leave his lungs. One down; four to go. The next guy swung at me, and I picked him up and body slammed him. One of them came up behind me and grabbed my arms. I lifted my legs up and caught the one coming to help right in the chest. Then I reverse head-butted the guy who held my arms. I could hear his nose crunch as he hit the ground. That left Jimmy Earl and me. Jimmy Earl didn't want any more; he put it in "B" for boogie and started running.

I quickly made my way back to my car and put my sweats on over my trunks and made my way home. It was a good night.

As I lay in my bed that night, I was sure Miss Edna would have been very proud. "The only thing necessary for the triumph of evil is for good men to do nothing." I was very glad that God gave me the ability to do something.

CHAPTER TWELVE
SCARS

S cars are caused by wounds. I was once thrown from a horse into a tractor. I have a scar on my leg that always reminds me of that event. You usually carry scars with you until you die.

When I was a little boy, my mom became very ill and had to go to a hospital for a lengthy stay. Because my dad was a long-distance truck driver and could not stay home to take care of me, I was put into the home of relatives.

Usually, we think of relatives as those who love us almost as much as our parents. But that is not always the case. It wasn't in my situation.

I was an only child for ten years until my sister was born. I did not feel close to any of my cousins. My closest friend was Miss Edna. Even though she was much older than me, I enjoyed her company more than anyone my own age. I also have a childhood friend I've kept up with throughout my life. His name is Mike. Mike could always make me laugh like no one else. He was and continues to be a great friend.

Besides my parents, Miss Edna, and Mike, there were no other people I could go to during difficult times. Even though that was true, I have always felt very fortunate. Some people have absolutely no one they can call a true friend.

It was very difficult to pack my bag and be sent to my relatives' home. They were not compassionate and always made me feel like I was a burden to them. There was no room for error with them. That is a very difficult situation to be put in as an adult, much less a child.

I was so thrilled the day my mom got out of the hospital and my dad came to pick me up. I didn't think I would ever quit hugging my mom.

Things continued to go well for a couple of weeks, but then my mom became ill again and had to go back to the hospital. When my dad told me that my mom had to go back to the hospital and I would have to go back to my relatives to stay, I burst into tears and ran out the door.

I ran to the only place I could find comfort from a human—Miss Edna. When I got to her house, I could see her working in her flower bed. She could hear my footsteps and turned around about the time I ran into her with my arms open.

When I got to her, I hugged her and cried. At first she didn't say a thing. She just held me and hugged me and ran her hand over my head. I continued to cry as I hugged her tightly. She knew something was terribly wrong but sensed I needed to cry a little more.

"What's wrong, child? You can tell Miss Edna."

"My mom is sick again and has to go back to the hospital. My dad is going to take me back to my relatives. I don't want to go back there."

"They are your relatives, child; they love you."

"No, they don't love me. They were mean to me. They didn't want me there when I was with them the last time."

"Precious child, I am so sorry they treated you that way. I can't imagine why someone would treat anyone that way, much less a precious child. But I love you, and your folks love you a whole bunch. You're going to be all right."

"Life isn't fair, Miss Edna."

"Oh, yes, child. Life is fair. We all have our difficulties in one way or another. No one is excluded from all of the hardships in life, no one."

"But I won't get to see you, and I miss you so much while I'm with them."

"Child, listen to me. You are going to have to be strong. Your mama needs you to be strong. She probably feels very bad that she has to go back to the hospital. Your daddy needs you to be strong. He probably feels bad that he can't stay home and take care of you. God promised us He would never leave us or forsake us. God will be with you, child, and you will be in my prayers every day."

I could hear someone behind me call my name. It was my dad's voice: "We need to go, son."

Miss Edna bent down and looked me in the eyes and placed a necklace around my neck. "My daddy gave me this necklace when I was a little girl. Every time I grab the cross on this necklace, I think of God and how He blessed me with such a wonderful daddy. I think of my daddy, and it makes me feel better. Now every time you grab the cross, you can think of how much God loves you. And you can also think of me. I'll be right here when you get back."

My dad picked me up and took me back to my relatives. In front of my dad, they acted like they were glad to see me and told me to put my bag in the extra bedroom. I hugged my dad and went to put my bag away.

Things did not change. They made me feel like a leper while I was with them. They said cruel things about my mom and dad when they didn't know I was listening.

Every time I felt alone, I grabbed the cross like Miss Edna said. It did bring me comfort. I still carry the scars from those days. I guess that's why I was so shattered when a child and family representative from the state came to see me about two little girls in our church.

The girls hadn't been attending very long. Their relatives dropped them off every Sunday. The relatives did not attend our church; they simply dropped the two little children off in time for Sunday school and picked them up after church services.

I was in the parking lot the first Sunday they were dropped off. Sadly, I didn't know the story then, or I would have done more to help sooner.

Their mom and dad had been in a terrible car accident. Fortunately, the parents were going to be okay, but they would be in the hospital and rehab for a long time. The mom's only sister lived in our town and her home was the only place the children could stay.

The aunt seemed to be a nice lady. She was the one who dropped off the children every Sunday.

The child and family representative told me the man living with the aunt was suspected of physically abusing the children. A schoolteacher had noticed some marks and bruises on the two children and had alerted Child and Family Services.

While talking to the two children, the representative had found out they were attending our church. The children told him how much they enjoyed coming because they felt so welcomed.

The representative told me he didn't have enough concrete evidence to take the children out of that home. He asked me to keep a close eye on the children while they attended our services. I assured him I would do all I could to help.

When he left my office, I thought back to my situation as a child. I wasn't physically abused by my relatives, but my hurt was still very deep.

I swore when I became an adult I would always try to help if I ever ran into someone in the same situation.

I made a visit to the children's aunt's home. When the door opened and the children saw it was me, they ran with open arms. I hugged them and told them I was always so glad to see them. The aunt seemed very pleasant as she invited me inside.

"I just wanted to come by and say thank you for allowing the children to attend the church." I told her how wonderful the children were and asked if there was anything we could do for them.

"You can't make their mama and daddy better any quicker, can you?" I heard the man say as he came into the living room. "We got enough of our own troubles without having to take care of two little brats. But dropping them off at the church on Sunday does give us a little bit of time to ourselves."

You could see the children shudder when they heard his voice. I could see fear in their eyes as they watched him sit down on the couch.

"Sir, I really don't think that is a proper way to talk about the children's parents in front of them."

I looked at them and said, "Why don't you girls go play while we talk?"

They didn't need much encouragement to run out of the room. My heart sank as I watched them run. I could also see the disappointment in the eyes of the aunt.

"My wife and I would be more than happy to have the children come and stay with us. We have two little girls, and they would fit in perfectly," I offered.

The man obviously was growing a little agitated as he rose to his feet and said, "Well, the only good thing is that we get a check every month for taking care of them, and that comes in handy. So, thanks just the same, and it's probably about time for you to be leaving, isn't it, Preacher?"

I didn't drive home after I left their house. I found a place where I could park to see where the man went when he wasn't at home. I would find the perfect place to help him with an attitude adjustment.

He was like most losers in his category. He had a favorite watering hole where he hung out. The place where he parked his car was a perfect location for The Masked Saint to make a visit. I would be watching, waiting to find the right time.

The following day was Sunday. I always tried to be in the parking lot to greet people as they arrived for church. I still do that even today.

When the aunt let the girls out of the car, they ran to me and gave me a big hug. After I hugged one of the girls, I put my hands on her shoulders to look her in the eye and tell her how happy I was to see her. However, when I touched her right shoulder, she grimaced with pain. I pulled her sleeve up and saw a big bruise at the very top of her arm.

"How did you hurt your arm, sweetheart?" She never answered me; she just looked down at the ground and walked away with her sister.

I looked up in time to make eye contact with the aunt. She obviously looked upset also. I didn't know her situation, but like a lot of folks, I guess she had made some bad choices in her life and didn't see a way out.

It was difficult for me to preach that day as I thought about those two precious little girls being abused by the man entrusted with their care and well-being. I would have to act soon to help with this situation.

The bars always closed at eleven p.m. on Sundays. If the man was there that night, I would be ready.

When I parked in a secluded spot, I could see the man's car was there. I was dressed and waiting for the right opportunity. I couldn't have planned it better. He was leaving before closing time and was headed toward his car. I put on my mask and made my way to the nearby shadow.

I stepped out of the shadow and grabbed him and threw him behind the building.

"Hey, man, what's your problem?" he said as he was getting up.

"Dirt bags like you are my problem. You do well hitting little girls. How do you do against someone your own size?"

"There's only one way to find out," he said as he made a swing at my head.

I grabbed his arm and put him on the ground so hard, it felt like the earth shook. He still needed a little bit more of an attitude adjustment. I picked him up and body slammed him for good measure.

I knelt down beside him and said, "If I ever learn of you laying a hand on those two little girls again, I will be back to talk with you once more. Do you understand me?"

He shook his head okay and said, "Please, no more. I won't touch 'em."

Fortunately, the girls didn't have to stay much longer. They were soon back with their mom and dad. But I'm sure the scars stayed with them for a lifetime.

CHAPTER THIRTEEN

DEALING
WITH TRAGEDY

love going to McDonald's. I love the smell of the coffee in the morning and the wonderful aroma of the freshly baked biscuits.

Every now and then, I love to stop by McDonald's on the way to the office. I always get the same thing: a plain biscuit, an egg biscuit, and a large Diet Coke.

Since I would be working mostly at the office doing sermon preparation that day, I decided to stop by and get "my usual."

A gentleman ahead of me was making his order. The young lady who was waiting on him had to ask him to repeat just about everything he said. She couldn't understand what he was saying. The man became annoyed with the young lady and insulted her loudly.

I snapped as I heard him say some pretty nasty things to the young lady. She had tears in her eyes as the man continued in his rant.

I touched the man on the shoulder and said, "Would you please stop being such a jerk? That young lady is probably sixteen years old, working for minimum wage. She can't understand what you are saying. So, speak slowly, get your order, and get out of line!"

"I'm sorry. I guess we have a communication problem," he said, as he quickly grabbed his order and made his way out of the building.

I guess I didn't look very Christian as I snapped at him. Rude people picking on those who are unable to respond always brings out the worst in me. I always try to treat young people working at fast-food restaurants like I would want someone to treat my child.

The young lady seemed very appreciative that someone had stuck up for her. She thanked me for defending her and was very prompt in getting my biscuits and Diet Coke.

I sat down to eat my breakfast and look at the sports section of the paper. I heard a familiar voice say, "Hello, Reverend."

It was Detective Harper. He was the detective who had come to the office inquiring about the wife-beating husband.

"Hello, Detective, how are things with you?"

"I'm keeping busy."

"Did you ever catch the guy who beat up the wife beater?"

"No, I haven't. As a matter of fact, I think he has been visiting some other less-than-reputable folks in our fair city."

"Well, I hope everything works out all right. By the way, why don't you come and visit our services one Sunday?"

"I might just do that, Reverend. Well, I've got to get my order and leave. Take care!"

I knew I could speed up this impromptu visit by inviting him to church. I was soon back to my morning paper.

I enjoyed eating my breakfast, drinking my Diet Coke, and reading. I usually go right for the sports section, but I couldn't help noticing an article on the front page. The article said there had been several reports of people's cars being vandalized in parking lots all over the city. I just shook my head, wondering why things like that had to happen.

My day went by pretty fast preparing a sermon and making a few visits. I couldn't wait to get home and spend some time with my family.

Right before we turned in for the night, my phone rang. Whenever my phone rings at that time of the night, it is never a good thing. It was the wife from one of my church families. They had been in an automobile accident and were at the emergency room.

I kissed my girls good-bye and left for the hospital. I prayed a quick prayer for the family as I drove. Tragedy usually gives very little warning when it strikes.

I had a little sister who only lived seven days. I remembered how my mom suffered through that difficult time. I remembered the well-meaning people who came by our house to offer their condolences.

One lady in particular said something memorable to my mom before she left the house: "Remember, honey, it was God's will."

As a little boy, I couldn't imagine a God who would be so mean. I certainly didn't understand or comprehend what that woman had told my mother. Fortunately, Miss Edna had a way of making more sense out of things than anyone else I knew.

I remember running to her house in tears that day, sharing with her what the woman had told my mother. Miss Edna pulled me up close to her and hugged me. She had big tears in her eyes as she comforted me.

"Child, I'm sure that woman felt she was helping your mom—even though she didn't. God ain't mean, child. God created a perfect world and put two perfect people in a perfect garden in perfect surroundings. Unfortunately, they chose to sin. When sin entered the world, it brought with it sickness and death. Unfortunately, sickness and death touches the lives of the innocent as well as the guilty."

I don't remember everything she shared with me on that day, but I have always remembered those words. Those words have helped me to be a comfort to many people over the years.

I was so thankful things went well at the hospital. The family had their share of injuries, but they would be okay.

As I walked into the parking lot, I had to get my bearings as I tried to remember where I had parked my car.

I didn't remember the parking lot being so dark when I went in. Then, I noticed that someone had broken the lights in that area of the parking lot.

As I made my way toward my car and my eyes adjusted to the darkness, I could see a couple of images on the side of one of the cars. Two men in dark clothing were attempting to break into one of the cars. We noticed each other about the same time.

I didn't have my mask on, and I certainly didn't have time to change, but I had to do something. I decided to take the initiative. I ran toward them and jumped up on the hood of one of the cars and did a flying dropkick right into the chest of one of the men. He bounced back into a car and hit the ground. As the other man ran toward me, I dropped down and backflipped him. That hurts when it's done on concrete.

I looked in their bags and saw things they had taken out of cars in the parking lot. There was also something I could use to tie them up. Fortunately, it was dark enough they would never be able to identify who they had fought with.

I stopped at a pay phone and called 911. I told them there were two suspicious-looking people in the parking lot of the hospital and hung up.

I made my way back to my house. It was the "wee" hours of the morning. It was so good to lie down and know the injured family would be okay. It was also good to know that maybe there wouldn't be as many cars being vandalized in the city.

CHAPTER FOURTEEN
FEAR

hen I was small, I was no different from any other kid; I had my share of fears. I was afraid of the dark and also had a fear of heights. I certainly had fears when I was very sick in the fourth grade.

One day when I was at Miss Edna's, she noticed I was too preoccupied for a little boy. I seemed to be in a whole different world, staring off and not saying much. When she asked me questions, she would have to ask me twice because I didn't hear her the first time.

"What's wrong with you, child? You seem to be somewhere else today."

"Oh, I'm okay, Miss Edna. I just have a lot on my mind."

"You're way too young to have that much on your mind. Why don't you tell Miss Edna what's on your heart?"

"You won't laugh at me, will you?"

"Child, even if I did laugh, I wouldn't be laughing at you or your circumstances."

"Are you afraid of dying, Miss Edna?"

"Precious child! What would make you ask something like that?"

My grandmother had died several months before. I cried and was very sad. It was the first time I could ever remember seeing my dad cry. I felt I had gotten over it, but then a beloved member of the church died, and it brought back all those memories. And for the first time in my life, I thought about dying.

"A man in our church died. I guess I had never thought much about it, but I just can't get it off my mind today. I'm afraid to die."

"Child, we serve a great God. He's promised never to leave us or forsake us. He loved us so much He sent His only Son into the world so that we could be saved. One day, when you understand, you're going to invite Him into your heart to save you. But if you did die today, God would take you straight to heaven to be with Him because you ain't old enough to know better."

"I'm also afraid of the dark. I hate opening my closet door in the morning because I think there's a monster just waiting to get me."

"Child, I want you to listen to me. Our greatest fears are usually never realized."

"What does that mean, Miss Edna?"

"It means the things we usually worry about the most don't happen."

I never forgot those words. As a matter of fact, I have shared them with many people I have counseled over the years.

It had been a long day, and I was very tired. I was up late the night before, helping a family that had experienced a great tragedy. When I got home, I couldn't sleep, so I worked out hard and went out and ran four miles. It helped me to sleep; I just didn't get much of it.

When I got home, I sat in my chair and read the sports section. The sports section always helped me to relax. That is, until I saw an ad announcing that wrestling was coming to the arena in the closest big city. Wrestling wasn't unusual; it was who would be on the card that caught my attention: The Grappler.

I have to go back to the time when I was a youth minister to explain why it was so bothersome.

I have to tell you; I was not a very good youth minister. It wasn't my calling. I wasn't lazy; I just didn't know how to be a good youth minister. I didn't know how to deal with some of the problems a youth minister deals with.

I also didn't get along with the senior pastor like I wanted to. He was pretty arrogant and self-centered. I didn't feel he was trying to help me. When he spoke to me, he seemed to speak down to me.

I had been having a problem with a young lady in my youth group. I went to the pastor for his counsel. But because she was the daughter of one of the prominent members of the church, he refused to deal with it or help me deal with it.

One morning, I went in to talk with him and to beg for his help. When I got through, I finished with this statement: "Pastor, this doesn't work if we don't support each other."

His words were, "You know, Chris, you are absolutely right. So, why don't we just consider you gone right now?"

I walked out of that meeting with no job, and my wife had just given birth to our first child. I had to support my family, so I called a promoter and asked if I could go back to wrestling full-time. He signed me up for a match that very night.

I would be working against The Grappler. He was a big, rough individual. I had never met him, but I had heard a lot about him. He was known to take advantage of young guys new to the business. He was also known for putting some guys out of wrestling because of the injuries they sustained at his hands.

I felt confident in my skill because I had been trained by one of the very best. I wasn't any more nervous on that night than any other night.

I got to the arena early to warm up and relax, trying to put it out of my mind that I had been fired from my first job in the ministry. How would I be able to go to another church? Would being fired be held against me when I tried to find another church? I had to quiet my mind and concentrate on the match.

When I got into the ring, he seemed to look straight through me. When the match started, he kicked me in the stomach and threw me into the turnbuckle. It felt like my back would explode from the collision. Then he wrapped my leg around the second rope and twisted upward. I felt my knee pop.

Even though he was supposed to win the match, it was supposed to end the way the promoter had called it. He was supposed to use his finish hold on me and pin me.

I couldn't move because of the knee, so I rolled outside the ring. When the referee jumped outside the ring, I pulled him down and told him my knee was busted and I couldn't finish the match. He jumped back in the ring and counted me out and raised the hand of The Grappler.

I lay there on the floor in tremendous pain. The paramedics were there quickly, and I was soon on my way to the hospital.

The damage was extensive. I had torn my ACL and my MCL. I was in the hospital for several days after the surgery. The longer I was in the hospital, the more bitter and angry I became. Out of the big church I had served, only one person came to visit me.

We had no insurance, and I had no job, and my wife had just given birth to our first child. I certainly wouldn't be wrestling for a long time.

Because of our financial situation, we lost our home and car—but that wasn't the biggest embarrassment. We also had to move in with my folks because we didn't have anyplace else to go. We had to have help from them just to make it.

I remember the first Sunday after moving back in with my folks. I was sitting on the couch with my leg in a cast. My wife walked into the living room, laid our baby girl on the couch, and picked up little dresses, seeing which one she would dress her in.

Even though I knew what she was doing, I still asked, "What are you doing?"

"I'm getting our baby girl ready for church. I'm going to find a church somewhere around here to attend."

"Church?" I said in disgust. "After what they did to me?"

My wife had had enough. She turned around, also in disgust, and said, "Chris, your problem is that you have had your eyes focused in the wrong place. People will let you down every time. God hasn't let you down. Look what they did to Jesus, and He was perfect. Why do you think you are so special? Your problem is that you have had your eyes on people instead of God. He hasn't forsaken you, and He never will. And I'm not coming to your pity party."

Wow! She quickly dressed our baby and herself and headed out the door. I was left to sit there and think about all that she had said to me.

Sometimes, the truth really hurts when it hits home. Everything she said was true. When she came home, I was man enough to admit she was right. God had not forsaken me. I would get over my bitterness and pity and concentrate on getting well and going forward.

I did go forward. It took about a year for my leg to heal. I had a great doctor and a great therapist. With God's help and medical help, I was able to get in better shape than I had ever been before.

Now here it was, years later, and I still had fear in my heart. The fear was because of The Grappler. When I thought of him, my heart beat quickly. I had heard from some of my wrestling friends that I wasn't the last person he put in the hospital.

Even when I went to bed, as tired as I was, I couldn't sleep. I could see his face, just as clearly as on the night I wrestled him. I could hear my knee pop over and over again. I remembered all of the hardship I put my family through because of the injury. What could I do to get over this fear?

I thought back to my conversation with Miss Edna on the day she told me that our greatest fears were usually never realized. She told me the best way to deal with fear is to deal with it: "You've got to face your fears, child."

The next morning, I called the promoter in Tampa. We had always had a good relationship. He was glad to hear from me after so long. I told him I was now the pastor of a church. There was a long silence, but then he said, "You always were a little different from the other guys. I just never pictured you ending up as a pastor of a church."

He asked me what he could do for me. "I'm glad you asked me that. How many other shows in Florida will The Grappler be working in?"

"Well, I think we have a couple of more shows: one in Miami and one in Orlando."

"Are these dark matches (meaning they won't be shown on TV)?"

"The one in Miami is a not being televised. Why do you ask?"

"I would like for you to do me a favor. Put me in the match against The Grappler in Miami. You don't even have to pay me."

"Are you sure about this? Are you in shape?"

"I'm in great shape, and yes, I am absolutely sure about this."

"Not too many guys want to get in the ring with him, but I'll see what I can do."

I told him I would wear my old outfit and work under my old name. And I also asked him not to tell anyone what I was doing and where I was living. I knew I could trust him to keep my confidence.

Fortunately, the match was on a Friday evening. It worked well for me. I could drive to Miami on Friday morning, wrestle that night, and drive back on Saturday morning. There was only one problem: how would I share this decision with my wife?

The next day, I asked my wife if we could have lunch together. I wanted to be honest with her, but I didn't want her to worry about me. If I told her I was going to be getting back in the ring against the guy who put me in the hospital, I knew she wouldn't be supportive of that.

"Honey, I know we always have our Friday night fun night, but I can't this week."

"Why not?" she said, looking disappointed.

"Do you trust me?"

"I haven't had another date since I was sixteen years old. I've been with you through the good times and the bad. Is there any reason you can think of that would make me not trust you?"

"I have to take a trip to take care of something. I'll be glad to talk to you about it after I get back. Just please trust me until then, and I'll tell you about it."

"Okay, honey, I trust you."

The drive to Miami actually went more quickly than I thought it would. I thought about every tough match I had ever had. I thought about my training and about every conversation I ever had with Miss Edna. The time flew by.

When I got to the match, it was good to see some of my old friends from the business. We talked about our families. Most of them didn't push me about what I was doing now. I just told them I was working in Central Florida.

The promoter came into the dressing room to talk with me about how the match was supposed to end. I had my instructions. Only this time, I really didn't have to follow those instructions.

Usually, if you did not do it the way the promoter called it, you wouldn't be working very long. They were very particular about wrestlers following the way they called the match. Only this time, I didn't care if I worked again. This was my last match.

The time finally came for my match: me against my fear. As I walked into the arena to the screaming, passionate fans, it brought back a lot of memories. I always loved the smell of the arena.

The ring looked to be a mile away as I made my way there. I jumped to the side of the ring and leaped over the top rope. I didn't realize how much I had missed doing that.

The music played, and I turned around to see The Grappler coming through the curtain. He screamed at the fans and made gestures as he made his way to the ring. My heart beat quickly. He made his way into the ring and stared at me like he did on that night several years before. He was shouting something at me, but I couldn't hear what he was saying.

The bell rang, and the match started. When we locked up, he said, "Been a long time, boy. Where you been?" as he pushed me back into the ropes.

We locked up again. Only this time, I arm dragged him to the mat and said, "I've been looking forward to this night."

I pulled him up with an armlock and walked him over to the corner of the ring. I gave him a push as I released him. When we locked up next, he kicked me in the stomach and gave me a forearm to the head. Not only did I have trouble catching my breath, but I also was seeing stars. He quickly picked me up and body slammed me. This match wasn't going the way I had hoped.

He grabbed me by the mask and began pulling me up off the mat. Again, he body slammed me and gave me a kick to the stomach to boot. Then he grabbed me and walked me back into the ring ropes. He threw me into the opposite ropes and close-lined me across the chest.

Again, he grabbed me by the mask and walked me back into the corner. It was almost like it was happening in slow motion as he picked my leg up and wrapped it around the second rope. As he grabbed my boot to give my leg a good yank, he said, "Let's see how strong that leg is now."

Only this time, my leg didn't pop. Before I ever got back into the ring after my first match with him, I had a steel leg brace made that would keep my knee from being twisted like it was before.

He looked shocked when he realized that my knee was not going to twist like it did in our first match. I gave him a little "love tap" to the side of the head that stunned him.

Then, I backed him into the corner and took his leg and put it over the second rope. I grabbed his foot to give it lift, but I just stood there, staring at him. I could easily do to him what he had done to me years ago, but I knew that would be revenge, and revenge belonged to God. My fear had diminished.

I looked him in the eye and said, "I could hurt you like you hurt me, but I'm not going to do it. But you need to remember this night. You got a tremendous break. You need to change your ways."

I quickly body slammed him and got him in the figure four leg lock. With the steel brace on my knee and the strength of my legs, there was no way he would break the hold. He had no choice but to concede. I walked out of the ring victorious. The ref had a shocked look on his face because he knew I was supposed to put The Grappler over.

When I got back to the dressing room, the promoter was screaming at the top of his lungs, asking what in the world I was doing not following his instructions. I just smiled and said, "Sorry, boss. It didn't cost you anything."

Even though I had planned to stay the night in Miami, I was so pumped about my victory, I was able to drive all the way home. I arrived home about four o'clock in the morning. The dog was barking at the top of his lungs, waking everyone in the house.

I quickly shouted, "It's me. It's only me."

My wife wasn't too happy with me scaring her, but she seemed glad to see me home, especially not knowing what was going on when I left. I started getting ready for bed, but she stopped me and asked if I would sit down and tell her what was going on.

I sat on the edge of the bed and said, "I knew you wouldn't want me to do what I did tonight, so that's why I asked you to trust me."

"What did you do?"

"I got back into the ring tonight to deal with my fear and my bitterness. I wrestled the man who put me out of work for a year."

"Are you okay? Did you get hurt again?"

"No. I'm fine. I had planned to hurt him like he hurt me, but I couldn't do it. But I did win the match and dealt with a lot of demons."

"Don't ever do that to me again, Chris. You could have been hurt, and you could have jeopardized our safety as a family."

"You are right, honey. I shouldn't have done it, but I'm glad I did. You don't have to worry about me doing it again."

Miss Edna was right, "Our greatest fears are usually never realized."

CHAPTER FIFTEEN

CHRISTMAS BLESSINGS

C hristmas is my favorite time of the year. People just seem to be nicer during Christmas than any other season. I love having all the family together; I love the meals and the smell of the house on Christmas morning.

Our Christmas tradition actually starts Thanksgiving weekend. We always set up our tree and put up all the lights on the Saturday after Thanksgiving. We watch every Christmas movie that plays on TV. Our favorite is *It's a Wonderful Life,* with Jimmy Stewart.

Our second baby was born in 1982. She was just as precious as the first one. Carrie was our oldest, and Annie was our baby. We couldn't have asked God to give us two better young ladies.

It was always important for my wife and me to teach our children how blessed they were. Every year, our church would help as many poor families as we could to provide Christmas gifts for their children.

I know the reason for Christmas is the birth of Jesus. I always taught that to our girls.

However, when children are in school, they hear the other children talk about what they are going to get for Christmas. It broke my heart for any child not to receive gifts at Christmas.

When I would take gifts and food to families who needed help, I would often take my children with me. I wanted them to see how blessed they were. And I also wanted to see them grow up learning to be benevolent to those who were not as blessed as they were. It was something I learned from Miss Edna when I was a child.

It was getting close to Christmastime when I was in the fifth grade. All the kids were excited because it was close to the Christmas break, and we would have two whole weeks off from school. We were also excited about the gifts we would be receiving on Christmas Day.

One day when I went by to see Miss Edna, she and Mr. Williams were putting up Christmas decorations. Mr. Williams had cut his own tree down; it was a beautiful tree, and Miss Edna was putting out her favorite decorations. I was trying to help her, following her instructions carefully.

"You excited about Christmas, child?"

"Yes, ma'am, I can hardly wait!"

"You know, not every little boy and girl get something for Christmas. I always try to find someone in need and help him. You gonna help someone this year?"

"I don't know anyone who needs help."

"All you have to do is look, child. They're all around you. You look for sad faces, for children who don't smile when the other children are talking about gifts."

"I've never thought much about it, but even if I could find someone, I can't buy him a gift."

"You find him, child, and you and Miss Edna will find the gifts."

The next day at school, when the kids were talking about what they were getting for Christmas, I did look and Miss Edna was right. I saw a couple of sad faces; there were no smiles.

When I went to Miss Edna's that day, I told her about the two children I noticed. She said that since she and Mr. Williams didn't have any children, she would buy for them. Since that day, I have continued to look for the sad faces. She is still right. They are all around us.

On this particular day, when I was taking some gifts and food to a young couple who had come by the church asking for help, I noticed a brown pickup truck speeding down the street. One of the men in the truck was holding up a gift in red paper. I didn't realize it then, but I would be glad I noticed the truck and the man holding the gift.

One of the families we had already helped lived across the street from this young couple. They were pulling into their driveway as I was pulling into their neighbors' drive.

After I delivered the gifts and food with my little girls' help, we were making our way back to the car when I heard crying. The man from across the street was standing in his driveway with his head down. His wife and children were in the house crying.

"Are you okay?"

"No, Pastor, I'm not. Someone broke into our home and stole the gifts from under our tree. They took our TV and a gun my grandfather left me. Pastor, they took my baby girl's presents."

Then it hit me. I remembered delivering those gifts. I remembered a gift in red paper. The men in that brown pickup truck had stolen those gifts.

I went to the police station to report what had happened. Detective Harper shared with me that there had been several homes hit in that area. It made my blood boil to think someone would steal gifts from poor families. I didn't tell Detective Harper that I had seen the brown truck. If there was any way I could take care of this one, I was sure going to try.

The next evening, I went riding around that neighborhood and the neighborhoods close by, trying to find the brown truck. I was about to give up for the night when I saw the nose of a brown truck parked backwards in a driveway. I pulled on ahead and parked my car. I was watching the house out of my rearview mirror.

Sure enough, two men came out of the back of the house with a couple of bags over their shoulders. They had hit another house.

I had my sweats on over my tights and boots. My mask was in my bag. I would follow the men. I'm sure they would lead me to where they were hiding all the gifts they had stolen. That's where I would take care of business.

They drove to the other side of town. I'm not used to "tailing" someone, so I stayed as far back as possible so they wouldn't be suspicious. They finally made their way to a little house at the end of a street that didn't have very many houses.

I found a place to park my car so it wouldn't be noticed and made my way to the house where the thieves were. I decided to wait for them to come back outside.

It didn't take them long before they came back outside. They were startled when I stepped out of the shadows.

"It always sickens me when I find people like you. You don't even care that you have ruined Christmas for children and their folks."

"What in the heck are you talking about? We haven't done anything to anybody."

"Not only are you thieves, but you're liars too."

One of the men grabbed a piece of pipe laying up against the house and began walking towards me. The other man was looking for something he could pick up and use for a weapon.

As the first man ran toward me, I dropped down and did a drop toehold. He went flat on his face, and the pipe went forwards out of his hand. I quickly gave him a shot to the back of the neck. He was out for the count.

I picked the piece of pipe up to protect myself from the second man. When he tried to hit me with the piece of wood he had found, I blocked it with the pipe. The piece of wood broke in two. I gave him a dropkick that sent him back into the house.

I tied the two men up and went inside to see if most of the stuff they had stolen was inside. I'm sure most of it was there. I saw the gift with the bright red paper. The gun they had stolen was leaning up against the wall. I'm sure everyone would be glad to get the gifts back.

I went to the first payphone I could find and called the police and told them where the men and the gifts were located. They always hate it when I don't give my name, but they didn't need my name. I'm sure they would be happy to have this case solved.

When I got home, my girls were busy helping their mom make Christmas cookies and watching a Christmas movie. I was glad I hadn't missed out on a great evening with my girls.

As I watched my girls with their smiling faces, it made me feel good that there would be other little boys and girls with smiling faces when their gifts were returned. I was glad I had followed Miss Edna's advice to look for the sad faces.

CHAPTER SIXTEEN
THE UNDERTAKER

The summers are usually difficult times for most small churches in Florida. There are usually a lot of folks gone every Sunday on vacation. The summers are difficult financial months for small churches because of this. Our church was no different.

When churches are behind in budget, they usually blame it on the pastor. I guess members have to have someone to blame. Even though I shouldn't have, I worried about those months.

Not only was this summer difficult because of all the folks on vacation, but we also had a couple of families move because they found jobs in other states. They had been very faithful tithers to our church. We were way behind on our budget, and the church people were getting anxious.

All I knew to do was to be faithful to God and depend on Him to help when I had done all I could do. Sadly, I tell you I still worried.

I remembered an afternoon like that with Miss Edna. I was worried about a test I had taken in school.

"Child, you look depressed. What's wrong with you?"

"I don't think I did very well on my math test today."

"Did you study for the test?"

"Yes, ma'am."

"Did you do the best you possibly could?"

"Yes, ma'am."

"Then you ain't got nothing to worry about."

"I still can't help it. What if I failed?"

"Child, let me ask you something. If you didn't do well on that test, would it be the end of the world?"

"No, ma'am."

"That's what you have to do, child. Ask yourself if what you are worrying about happened, would it be the end of the world? Would you still have a mama and daddy who love you? Would you still have a house to live in and food to eat? Would they throw you out of school?"

"No, ma'am, none of those things would happen."

"Then, you ain't got nothing to worry about. God is still on the throne. And you're going to be okay."

It was amazing how she could help me see things as they really were. I asked myself, *If we don't make budget, what is the worst thing that could happen?* I figured the worst thing that could happen would be for me to lose my church. If I did, would that be the end of the world? No, it wouldn't be the end of the world.

As long as I had my wife and girls, I was a very rich man. They couldn't take my girls away from me. If they let me go, there were other churches in need of pastors. Miss Edna was right; God had always provided.

Once when I was in seminary, things were a little tight financially. I was worrying about making ends meet.

I tried to wrestle whenever I could. But I was near the end of school, and I had a lot of work to do, so I was not able to wrestle as much as I needed to for our finances. I thought about Miss Edna's lesson on worry. I was counting on God to help me.

That night, I was wrestling in Dallas. Since it was Friday night, I took my girls with me. They didn't get to see Dad wrestle often because of school. This was a special night. I would wrestle in the first match, and then we would go out for pizza afterwards and have our Friday night fun night.

After my match, I went back to the dressing room to shower and get dressed. As I walked into the dressing room, the promoter was asking if anyone wanted to wrestle again. One of the wrestlers was unable to make it because of an injury. I sure needed the money, but who would I be wrestling against?

The promoter said the match would be against Mean Mark. Today, he wrestles as The Undertaker. I knew then this young man would be a star one day. He was six foot eight and weighed 315 lbs. I told the promoter I would do it.

I quickly asked one of the referees to go outside and let my wife know I would be working one more match. But I also told him to tell my girls we would still get pizza after the match. I didn't want to disappoint them.

I went out to the ring before Mark; the star always entered the ring last. I found my wife and girls in the crowd. I wanted to see their expressions when Mean Mark (The Undertaker) walked into the arena.

When the music started and Mark made his way into the arena, my girls started crying. My wife quickly picked up her purse and started looking through it like she had lost something.

The match started, and I wrestled twenty minutes against The Undertaker. It was a night to remember.

After pizza, we were on our way back to Fort Worth. I mentioned to my wife that I saw her pick her purse up quickly when she saw The Undertaker. I asked her what she was looking for.

She said, "I was looking for the checkbook to make sure we had paid the insurance premium."

Miss Edna was right. Would it be the end of the world if what I was worrying about happened? No. Our needs were met that night in Dallas because of the extra match. And God met our financial needs that summer at the church. It wasn't the end of the world.

CHAPTER SEVENTEEN
PRIDE

As I grew closer to the end of my ministry at my first church, I felt a new tension I had never felt before. Little things seemed to bother me more than in the past. Even though I was good at controlling my temper, there were moments when I felt close to losing it.

On one particular Sunday night after our evening service, we had a dessert fellowship. Those were usually popular events. People who normally did not attend the evening service would come back on Sunday evening for peach cobbler and German chocolate cake.

One of my deacons seemed to grow annoyed with me over the smallest things. It almost felt like whatever I did, he would find fault with me. This caused me considerable stress. The ministry is stressful enough without having one of your leaders giving you grief.

I was standing in the fellowship hall, talking with people and enjoying some of my favorite dessert. People were gradually leaving and heading home. The people who usually stayed were the ones who helped clean up. I noticed George as he was picking up plates and helping with the clean-up duties.

After I finished talking with some folks, I gobbled down my last piece of cake and took my last sip of coffee. I also helped with the clean-up duties. I looked at George and said, "How are things going for you?"

He said, "Things would be a lot better if I didn't have to deal with some of your faulty plans."

I knew what he was referring to. I had led the church to expand the parking lot, and it involved borrowing the money necessary for the completion of the project. That had annoyed George. He felt the church should never be in debt.

Normally, I would have walked away and tried to ignore his comments. But I was stressed and irritated and responded in a negative way.

My response was, "Well, George, if you would wake up and enter the real world, it wouldn't seem so faulty to you." And then I walked away.

It was not the right thing to do, and I knew it. But at least I didn't body slam him! I tried to rationalize my words and told myself I gave him what he deserved. We avoided each other after that incident.

When the church needed an exploratory committee to begin looking at the need for more space because of our tremendous growth, we needed to select the best people to serve. George was one of the people we needed.

When my chairman of deacons said, "I would like to suggest that we put George on this committee," I told him I would not allow that to happen. Little did I know, George had confided in my chairman about our conversation.

After the meeting, my chairman, Bill, said, "Pastor, I know you and George are having some difficulties, but I really believe you shouldn't hold it against him. You know he is one of the most qualified people to serve on this committee."

I did know he was one of the most qualified people. But my pride would not allow me to look beyond my feelings to make the right decision. I simply responded to Bill, "This decision belongs to me, and George is not going to serve on this committee."

I left the meeting and got in my car. I could feel my blood pressure rising, thinking about what had just taken place. Of all people, I certainly shouldn't have acted the way I did.

I had taken my sweats, tights, boots, and mask to the church with me. I had planned to ride around and see if I could work off some of my stress after the meeting. But I knew I couldn't do anything with the right spirit that night.

I went to a little café that also had drive-up service to have a cup of coffee and try to settle my nerves. As I sat there, I thought about Miss Edna.

"Child, you seem a little irritated today."

"Why shouldn't I be? I found out that Sheila likes someone else. She's supposed to be my date for the spring dance."

"I thought your girlfriend's name was Patricia."

"No. I used to like Patricia, but I really like Sheila."

"Why don't you ask Patricia to go to the dance with you?"

"I can't do that. I wasn't very nice when I broke up with her."

"Child, listen to me. Pride is like a big rock hanging around our necks. It makes us do things we know we shouldn't do. If you mistreated Patricia, that was wrong. You need to get that straightened out. Your pride is keeping you from doing what is right."

She was right. It was pride. And it was pride that made me do something childish at that meeting.

My thoughts were interrupted by a man screaming at a woman in a car at the end of the row I was on. I turned just in time to see him slap the woman hard across her face. My blood boiled at seeing him.

I quickly surveyed the situation, wondering how I could help that woman. Before I could put my thoughts together, the man opened the car door and began walking to the bathrooms located behind the café. That was my opportunity. I went around to the back of the building, took my sweats off in the shadows, and put on my mask. I could enter the bathroom from the side without being seen.

I made the change and went inside. I was careful to make sure no one saw me and also checked to see if anyone else was making his way to the bathrooms. The coast was clear.

When I entered the bathroom, the man was walking out of the bathroom stall. He looked shocked as he saw me. He also became nervous very quickly.

"I thought I would give you an opportunity to slap someone your own size."

"I don't want any trouble, man. My business with my girlfriend is no business of yours."

"I make it my business when I see people who can't defend themselves being abused. You have no business hitting a woman, you spineless jerk."

"I won't do it again; I promise you."

Normally, I think I would have tried to find a way to get the man to take a shot at me, but maybe he was being honest.

"I'm going to give you a break you don't deserve. But you better thank God tonight when you go to sleep that you didn't get a slap from me."

I turned around to walk out of the bathroom. The coward hit me hard between the shoulder blades. It's amazing, but when I'm "pumped," I don't feel the pain I might normally feel.

I turned around in time to block his next blow. I gave him a forearm smash, sending him crashing into the bathroom stall. I picked him up and gave him a good slap across the face. He was dazed.

I grabbed him by his shirt and pulled him up close to my face and said, "Too bad you didn't take the break I gave you. If I ever see you hit another woman, you'll get worse than this little experience. Do you understand me?" He shook his head and slumped to the floor.

I carefully made my way out, put my sweats back on, and walked back to the car. No one seemed to notice my little trip to humble the jerk.

As I drove around, I continued to think about what had happened at the meeting. I also thought again about Miss Edna's words: "Pride is like a rock that hangs around our necks, making us do things we know we shouldn't do."

I drove to Bill's house. When Bill answered the door, I said, "Bill, I'm sorry to drop by unannounced, but I want you to know you were absolutely right tonight. I'm going to George and get things right. George will serve on the committee. I just needed to share that with you before I go to see George."

"Thank you, Pastor. You're doing the right thing. I'm proud of you."

"Thank you, Bill. I wish it hadn't happened."

I drove to George's house and got things right. George was very gracious and even apologized to me for what he had said at the fellowship.

It sure felt good to get that rock off my neck.

CHAPTER EIGHTEEN
BETRAYAL

Since I had come to pastor this small church, we had been very blessed. The church was no longer small. We had grown to two Sunday morning services. We had built a new educational building and a new office complex.

My secretary, Mrs. Read, had been with me from my first day. She was a very good secretary, but she made her share of mistakes. I just never pointed them out to her. After all, we all make mistakes. She had gone from working twenty hours a week to full time shortly after I came to the church.

We also had a maintenance man named Roy. He was responsible for cleaning the buildings.

The church had also hired a full-time administrator by the name of John Walters. John handled the finances of the church and also worked with the committees. He was very gifted in what he did, but he had no personality or people skills.

The church had also called a young man to serve as minister of music and youth, Jason Kinders. A search committee had found the young man. It certainly would not have been my choice in calling him. There was just something about him that gave me a great uneasiness.

He sang like a cow with stomach trouble. He was always singing solos in services. It was a great embarrassment to me when he sang. I didn't think he was a standout youth minister either, but I had to work with the hand I had been dealt.

The day came when I had to tell Jason I didn't want him singing every Sunday. He was not very happy with me, but I didn't understand *how* upset he was with me.

He really needed to concentrate on our youth, who would be taking an out-of-state trip the following week. Our youth were all excited about going to Tennessee. They were excited about the trip, but they were also excited about going to a state where it was going to be very cold. Florida doesn't get much cold weather. The youth were excited about the possibility of seeing snow.

With the youth gone, I didn't have to worry about Jason for a whole week. And I didn't have to listen to him sing for a whole week.

I was at the church the morning our youth and chaperones left for Tennessee. After seeing them off, I needed to work on several things in the office. Before I could get started, Mrs. Read interrupted to tell me one of my members needed to see me.

Mr. Murray was one of my senior adults. He was a sweet man who had recently lost his wife of fifty years. Even though he had gone through some rough times, he always had a smile on his face. Today, though, he looked to be pretty distraught about something.

"Mr. Murray, it's good to see you. What can I do for you?"

"Pastor, I don't know what this world is coming to. I don't know what to do."

"Can you tell me what's wrong?"

"I was walking my dog last night, and a man held me up in my own neighborhood. Can you believe that, Pastor? He took the watch my grandfather gave me and all the cash I had on me."

"Did he have a gun?"

"Yes, and he was a big fella."

"Did you call the police?"

"Yeah, I called 'em. Detective Harper came out to see me, but I don't have great confidence they are going to do anything. Oh, I know Detective Harper is a good man, and he'll try to do the best he can, but the police hardly ever patrol our neighborhood."

"How did you describe the man to Detective Harper?"

"Well, he was a big fella, like I said. He had a tattoo on his left forearm. He had a scar over his eye and a crooked nose. That's about it."

"Well, I'm sure Detective Harper will do all he can to catch the man. But why did you come to tell me about it?"

"My only daughter lives in New York. If something happens to me, I want to make sure someone knows where I keep my valuables. I have a safe in the floor right under my bed. Here's the combination. I knew I could trust you, Pastor. If anything ever happens to me, please make sure my daughter gets this."

"I'm hoping and praying nothing ever happens to you. But I'll be glad to keep this for you."

After Mr. Murray left, I started back to work on the things that had been piling up, but I couldn't get it off my mind that someone could be robbed in his own neighborhood. I was also glad I had the description of the man who robbed Mr. Murray.

On my way home that evening, I drove over to the next city to a pawnshop. I figured if the man who robbed Mr. Murray tried to pawn the watch, he would probably take it to the next town. I described the watch to the man at the pawnshop and asked if he had seen it.

"You're too late. I've already sold it."

I didn't worry about the person who bought it. I figured the owner had to keep records, and the watch could be tracked down. I was concerned about the man who sold it to him.

"Was it a big fella with a tattoo on his left forearm?"

"Yeah, it was. He also had a scar over his eye."

"Did you happen to get any information about this man?"

The man looked through his records and finally pulled out a piece of paper. I was amazed; it had his name and address. But I figured he probably gave the man a different name and a wrong address.

I was right. When I tried to find him, there was no such address. But I figured the man was probably not through. He probably targeted older people.

As the week went by, each night I would drive through different neighborhoods. I especially traveled the neighborhoods with a large senior adult population. Each night went by without my seeing the man.

Our youth returned from their trip to Tennessee. They were full of stories about the places they visited and the weather. Sadly, they never saw snow.

I talked with Jason about the trip to see if everything had gone okay. He was pretty distant in his responses, but from everything he shared, I was thankful it seemed to go well.

That day I was at the office until dark. I had one more neighborhood to visit. I put my tights and boots on and wore my sweats over them. I was always prepared, just in case.

As I rode through the neighborhood, it was obvious there was very little activity. I was just about ready to give it up for the night when I saw a side street that was also a dead-end street. It wasn't lit very well. I could see what looked like two figures in the shadows. It might not be anything, but then again, it wouldn't hurt to take a look.

I found a place to park my car and made my way across a vacant field to the street where the two figures were. Sure enough, there was the "big fella" Mr. Murray had described to me. He had a gun pointed at an elderly man who was cleaning out his pockets for the robber.

I quickly took off my sweats and put on my mask. I had never faced a man with a gun before. I would have to make sure that I planned my moves well. I couldn't give him a chance to point it at me; I would have to attack him.

It seemed the best thing to do would be to take a running start and dropkick him from the back. I took a deep breath and prayed for God's help—and that He would keep the elderly man safe. I ran towards the man and placed a dropkick firmly between his shoulder blades.

The gun fired, but thankfully, the bullet went into the ground. The robber went facedown into the dirt and the gun went flying out of his hand. As the man tried to stand up, I gave him a hip toss back to the ground and put my knee firmly in his back so he couldn't move.

I asked the elderly gentleman if he was okay. He said he was fine. I asked him if I could borrow his belt and used it to tie the robber's hands behind his back. As big as he was, he wouldn't be able to get back on his feet without help. That would do until the police got there.

"Sir, would you mind calling the police and telling them to come pick this guy up?"

"No, I don't mind. Thanks for your help. I guess you're the guy I've been reading about in the paper."

"I'm just a man who hates to see people taken advantage of."

"I'm glad you were here tonight."

"Me too, sir. Have a good night."

I quickly made my way back to my car and put my sweats back on and hurried home to my girls. I sure was glad the man had been caught and was hoping Mr. Murray would get his watch back.

When I got home, my chairman of deacons was just pulling up in my driveway.

"You been out running, Pastor?"

"You might say that, yes. What brings you out tonight?"

"Well, if you've got time, Pastor, I really need to talk with you."

"Sure. Come on in; we can talk in the den."

We made our way to my den, and my wife brought us a couple of glasses of iced tea.

"What's on your mind, Mr. Becton?"

"Pastor, Jason Kinders asked to meet with the deacons. He told us the entire staff was unhappy with your leadership. After he got through, Mrs. Read and John Walters also asked to meet with us. Mr. Walters made several accusations against you in a four-page letter. Mrs. Read said that one of the speaking engagements you were recently on didn't last as long as you were gone."

I asked Mr. Becton to get the rest of the deacons together. I would meet with them and answer all of the charges against me. After saying he would line it up, I walked him to the door.

My wife had a worried look on her face when I shut the door. I explained what Mr. Becton had shared with me. Even Roy, the maintenance man, had said bad things against me.

I thought back to a time when I was betrayed as a boy. I didn't know what to do or how to react. My best friend had told a lie about me.

Miss Edna said, "Child, if the Son of God was betrayed by man, we shouldn't think we're so special it wouldn't happen to us."

I once had an old pastor tell me, "Son, when you are in the ministry, it doesn't even have to be true. All they have to do is say it, and your ministry is over."

I met with the deacons and answered all of the allegations against me. Thank God there were no moral accusations. I also shared with the deacons that if Mr. Walters had shared it with them, he had probably shared it with the whole church.

Indeed, he had shared it with the church. He sent a letter to every member.

It had all started with Jason. He was so angry with me for asking him not to sing that he decided he would try to ruin me.

I told the deacons I would also answer the charges to the entire church on Sunday evening. After talking it over with my family and spending time in prayer, I felt the best thing for me to do was to resign.

God had richly blessed me at this church. Even though 99 percent of the people did not want me to leave, I felt it was the best thing for the church for me to leave.

It was a difficult thing to stand before the people and answer made-up allegations about my integrity, but I felt I had done a good job of answering everything in the letter and the other things said by the staff.

After I put out my resume, it didn't take long for a church in Orlando to contact me. God was moving us to a larger city and a larger church. I was also sure there would be many more opportunities to help people being mistreated.

"The only thing necessary for the triumph of evil is for good men to do nothing." When I moved to Orlando, I would do all I could to make sure evil did not triumph.

EPILOGUE

It was a great joy to write this book. I must tell you that the greatest joy of my life was the day I accepted Jesus Christ as my Savior. I became a Christian my first semester while attending Palm Beach Atlantic University in West Palm Beach, Florida.

I had never planned to go to college. I went because the young lady I was in love with went to this school. (She eventually became my wife.) I wanted to be near her.

The first Sunday I attended the First Baptist Church of West Palm Beach, I heard one of the greatest preachers I have ever heard, Dr. Jess Moody. When I listened to him preach, it was as if I was the only one in the building. The message of God spoke to my heart. All week long, I wondered how in the world that man knew I was going to be in church on that day.

Surely he wouldn't know I would come back the next week. When I went back the next Sunday, again, the message of God spoke directly to my heart.

Each week he gave an invitation to come forward and accept Jesus Christ as Savior, but I couldn't do it. Each day, the conviction of the Holy Spirit continued to grab my heart.

Finally, one night in my dorm room, I got down on my knees and asked Christ to forgive me of my sin and to come into my heart and save me. He gave me a joy and a hope that is eternal. He did not make me perfect; I still make mistakes. But I wouldn't change my decision on that night for anything in the world.

If you have never accepted Christ as your personal Savior, you can do that today. What must you do?

First, we must realize we are sinners; we cannot save ourselves. I know; I know. People in this day and age do not like to hear the word *sinner*. But the Bible says, "All have sinned and fall short of the glory of God" (Rom. 3:23). And also, "For by grace you have been saved through faith, and that not of yourselves; it is the gift of God, not of works, lest anyone should boast" (Eph. 2:8-9).

The Bible also says, "For the wages of sin is death, but the gift of God is eternal life in Christ Jesus our Lord" (Rom. 6:23). And we are also given John 3:16: "For God so loved the world that He gave His only begotten Son, that whoever believes in Him should not perish but have everlasting life."

Why not call on the Lord in repentance, faith, and surrender right now? If that is what you would like to do, please pray this prayer with me:

Dear Lord, I know that Jesus Christ is Your Son. I know He died on the cross for my sin and was raised from the dead. I know I have sinned and need forgiveness. I am willing to turn from my sins and receive Jesus as my Savior and Lord. Come into my heart, Lord Jesus, and save me. Thank You, Lord, for saving me. In Jesus' name. Amen.

If you prayed that prayer, you are like an infant. You need to grow in your faith, and you also need to tell others about Jesus. We are his witnesses.

I encourage you to find a Bible-believing church in your area and talk to the pastor and tell him what you have done (accepted Christ as your Savior). Tell him you want to grow in your faith. He will help you in your new journey.

May God richly bless you as you serve Him!

ABOUT THE AUTHOR

 Chris Whaley grew up in Auburndale, Florida. He graduated from Palm Beach Atlantic University and Southwestern Baptist Theological Seminary. He has been married to his high school sweetheart, Verna Jacoby Whaley for forty years. Verna has been a high school math teacher for over thirty years. They have two daughters, Carrie Alyson and Kacie. They have five grandchildren, Dax, Charlotte, Richie, Wyatt and Harmony.

Chris wrestled for ten years (1978-1988) as The Saint. His last three years in wrestling was while he was a student at Southwestern Baptist Theological Seminary in Ft. Worth, Texas.

Chris serves on staff at the First Baptist Church in Orlando, Florida. Also serves as Chaplain for the Seminole County Florida Fire Department.

He loves speaking to people all across this great country, encouraging them to never give up and that we serve the God of a second chance. He is living proof of the second chance!